Elite: Docking is Difficult

Also by Gideon Defoe

The Pirates! in an Adventure with Scientists
The Pirates! in an Adventure with Whaling
The Pirates! in an Adventure with Communists
The Pirates! in an Adventure with Napoleon
The Pirates! in an Adventure with the Romantics

How Animals Have Sex

Elite: Docking is Difficult

GIDEON DEFOE

GOLLANCZ

LONDON

First published in Great Britain in 2014 by Gollancz
An imprint of the Orion Publishing Group
Orion House, 5 Upper St Martin's Lane,
London WC2H 9EA
An Hachette UK Company

A CIP catalogue record for this book is available
from the British Library.

ISBN (Cased) 978 1 4732 0130 9

1 3 5 7 9 10 8 6 4 2

Typeset by GroupFMG within BookCloud

Printed in Great Britain by Clays Ltd, St Ives plc

The Orion Publishing Group's policy is to use papers
that are natural, renewable and recyclable products and
made from wood grown in sustainable forests. The logging
and manufacturing processes are expected to conform to
the environmental regulations of the country of origin.

www.gideondefoe.com
www.orionbooks.co.uk
www.gollancz.co.uk

Other Elite books:

The original novella, and inspiration to us all:

Elite: The Dark Wheel, by Robert Holdstock

Available from Gollancz:

Elite: Wanted, by Gavin Deas
Elite: Nemorensis, by Simon Spurrier
Elite: Docking is Difficult, by Gideon Defoe

Available from Fantastic Books Publishing:

Elite: Reclamation by Drew Wagar
Elite: Lave Revolution by Allen Stroud
Elite: Mostly Harmless by Kate Russell
Elite: And Here The Wheel by John Harper
Elite: Tales From The Frontier by
15 authors from around the world

Available from other publishers:

Out of the Darkness by T. James
(Writer and Author Press)

For my mother, who was smart enough to buy
me a ZX Spectrum instead of a Commodore 64.
Nobody cares about your SID chip, losers.
TEAMCLIVE4EVUR

FED UP seeing the other guys and gals walk off with the BEST of EVERYTHING? Tired of your stupid JOB, of being overtaken by your peers, of lacking the *willpower* to get the things you want ... of being HALF ALIVE?

I know how it is BECAUSE I TOO was once an *under-achiever*. Hard to believe that of Cliff Ganymede – Best Selling Author; Decorated War Hero; Clinically-Recognised Supertaster; Zinc Magnate. But it's true. I dithered. I put stuff off. I failed to KNUCKLE DOWN. That's because I didn't know I was Elite. Now let me tell you a secret: *everybody* can be Elite. You're already ELITE! You just don't *realise* it yet. Elite. Say the word out loud with your *mouth*. Think about what it really means.

Each one of us has unlimited potential.
Life is there to be L-I-V-E-D[1]
I isn't a dirty word – put yourself first.
Time is now!
Each one of us has unlimited potential. (It bears repeating.)

Right at this moment you're at 'A' – sitting in your squalid habitation pod, lank hair stuck to a doughy, waxen face, wondering if the hole in your shapeless sweat pants is even bigger than the hole in your heart. Whereas I'm at 'B' – smelling of expensive shower gel, a Braben™ Real-Wool jumper enveloping my healthy, husky body, and a ready

1

supply of minced ortolans flowing direct from the brushed steel taps in my fully-featured kitchen. The question is: how do you get from A to B? The answer: via my three-day immersive ocular implant seminars, available on a host of topics to suit all needs. Popular examples include:

Find your inner Elite: Self Marketing & Neurotoxins
Find your inner Elite: Human Resources & How To Make Veiled Threats
Find your inner Elite: What Babies Can Teach Us About Innovating Agriculture
Find your inner Elite: A Guide To Dating Hot Unhappy Singles In Your Area
Find your inner Elite: Why Are These Changes Happening To My Body?
Find your inner Elite: Gas, Our Invisible Friend
Find your inner Elite: Conquer Social Media with Pie Charts

Remember: there's nothing *mostly harmless* about settling for less than you deserve.

Cliff Ganymede

---

[1]Now say the word 'LIVED' out loud. Think about what this word really means too: Love Interesting Valued Exciting D-A-Y-S![2]

[2]'DAYS' is another word worth saying out loud. Again, stop and ponder the actual meaning: Demand All Your S-U-C-C-E-S-S-S![3]

[3]Why not say 'SUCCESSS' out loud as well? You've probably already guessed this one : Seize yoUr Chances – Chances Equal Success So S-E-I-Z-E![4]

[4]Even if you're getting quite tired of saying words out loud, summon up one last burst of energy to think about what the word 'SEIZE' really means: Strength! Endurance! Intelligence! Zest! E-L-I-T-E![5]

[5](see above)

Chapter One

The President banged the dais with his brand-new faux-mahogany gavel and the entire population of Gippsworld – a hundred and nineteen citizens, tightly packed into the municipal centre's half-built holo-squash court – stopped arguing about pigs and methane for a moment and gazed up at him expectantly.

'Comrades – these are difficult times,' said the President, fixing the air above the front row with his most empathetic middle-distance stare. 'We find ourselves in the depths of a harsh economic winter. We find ourselves in a bind. And as the beady-eyed ice vultures of financial ruin circle overhead, we find ourselves at a crossroads.'

The President's demeanour was serious and solemn, so his audience nodded and pulled serious, solemn faces themselves, even though this wasn't news to anyone. A couple of the more easily impressed Gippsworldians murmured appreciatively about the 'vultures' line and said how good it was that the new president had a nice turn of phrase.

'Here on Gippsworld we hold a number of unenviable records. The lowest GDP for thirty parsecs. The most relentless precipitation. Smallest circumference for an inhabitable planetary body. Highest lead content.' The President paused. The crowd, perhaps expecting something a little more upbeat, shifted about uncomfortably. 'But I put it to you that we can also boast some other, better, though admittedly less tangible, statistics. Pluckiest population! Most indomitable spirit! Highest levels of vim and pep! I'm sure you can think of more besides.'

'Lowest rates of literacy?' shouted out Anatoly, who ran the Spaceport's cafeteria.

'Not that.'

'Highest infant mortality?'

'No, that's another bad one. My point is: we have not been dealt a great hand in the galactic poker game. But we can still play that hand like it was aces, or at least a pair of sevens or something. With that in mind, I'd like to present a short explanatory film I've put together, for which I also did the music.'

Somebody pressed a button and in swish KatzenbergKolor the film beamed out above the audience's heads, pointlessly detailing the planet's brief and underwhelming history that everyone had already learnt about back in primary school. It showed familiar three-generations-old footage of Gippsworld's discovery by the Hegarty Mining Conglomerate. It showed a cheery, oily-haired businessman planting a flag. It showed the excited headlines from the time:

A new gold rush out on the wild frontier!
The little planet with a BIG future!
Hegarty mining stock heading for the moon!

A Leading Scientist Of The Day appeared on an antique newsflash. 'Here is a world you might not give a second glance,' he said, polishing a model of an atom and beaming at the camera. 'A world so pint-sized you can wang a stone across it, if you've got a good arm. Yet it is blessed with a treasure as scarce as it is sensational. A sparkling deposit of Gooberite buried deep beneath the surface mud, like a clumsy cook's wedding ring lost inside an unappealing lasagne. Valuable – indeed vital – Gooberite! Our prayers have been answered.'

'It's something important to do with the manufacture of air-conditioning units,' said people in the know.

'It's the main ingredient of rusks,' said others.

'I think they use it in face-creams,' said a few more.

'An element as rare as hen's teeth!' boasted the Hegarty Mining Conglomerate's press office. 'Obviously beak dental-augmentation has come a long way in the last few decades, and that claim isn't what it used to be, but even so,' they added, in a slightly smaller font.

It was a resource no rational person could do without, everyone agreed on that. Amidst universal fanfare, plans for New Vladimir Putingrad were drawn up, a city and spaceport designed to match the boundless riches that would soon be flooding out of the ground. Work began on drilling a mineshaft through a mile of Gippsworld's tough, super-dense lead crust. A giant diamond drill-bit was shipped in from the carbon planet Rho Cancri V. The urbane, polo-necked presenter of the hugely popular *Architectural Exercises In Narcissism* show was on hand to record all the triumphs and innovations. A thousand breathless articles banged on about 'the raw ingenuity of man' and 'the towering resourcefulness of our modern industrial age' and 'the sheer Ayn Randian wonder of it all'.

Then, three months into the project, Lansbury Five – newly discovered in the adjacent star system – turned out to have reserves of Gooberite as well. There were a few key differences between Lansbury Five and Gippsworld. The seas on Lansbury Five didn't turn your epidermis into a powdery residue. The sand on the beaches was actual sand rather than millions of microscopic parasites. It had better TV reception. But the most significant difference was that Lansbury Five's Gooberite, instead of being lodged in tiny quantities a mile underground, was piled up everywhere in great, big, easy-to-access mounds. Anybody equipped with a sunhat and a spade and a decent-sized bucket could collect as much as they fancied. A new set of headlines popped up.

Gippsworld weather turns out to be massive pathetic fallacy.

White elephant, man's hubris: the usual shambles.

When mixed with rendered animal fat, Hegarty mining stock makes for effective draught excluder.

More footage, set to less jaunty music than before, showed work on the New Vladimir Putingrad mineshaft grinding to an overnight halt. Investors chalked it up as a handy tax write-off. Engineers, used to an itinerant life, found some other planets to build giant walls or mega pipes or super sewers on. Only the obstinate, the insane, and the otherwise unemployable stayed put. They sat around in the dirt and discussed their diseases and their humanities degrees and their syndicated life-style columns and pretty soon a hundred years passed by.

'Ever since that fateful day, our little planet has had to rely on just two natural resources: our indigenous pigs,' – the President had to pause again, as at this all the pig farmers in the room cheered, whilst all the methane farmers booed – 'and our methane.' At this point all the methane farmers cheered and all the pig farmers booed. Ninety percent of Gippsworld's inhabitants farmed either pigs or methane and they didn't rate each other highly. The methane farmers thought the pig farmers were uppity. The pig farmers thought the methane farmers had womanish hands.

'But margins for these products are low, and getting lower all the time,' the President continued, graver than ever. 'Following current trends,' – a sad-looking graph flashed up – 'our way of life will be unsustainable in a few short

6

years. Yet we have not been idle in trying to tackle this crisis. No indeed. As you may be aware, we recently spent our world's entire pension fund on the construction of a gigantic advertising hoarding, which – to be frank – hasn't really panned out.'

The Gippsworldians looked miserably up through the hole in the municipal centre's roof to where the three-mile-wide screen hung, static and black, stuck to the side of an enormous zeppelin sat in futile geostationary orbit. Half a billion credits, but it had never been switched on. Corporations had shown little interest in what the newly formed Advertising Ministry's expensive brochures described as '*a unique mega-wattage marketing opportunity; your chance to really connect with people, day or night*'. The corporations cited the lack of anybody on Gippsworld worth connecting with; a flaw that the population grudgingly admitted seemed sort of obvious in retrospect. A few companies had said they'd be happy to use the giant floating advertising site so long as they didn't have to pay anything. When the Gippsworldians asked what was in it for them, the companies had just shrugged and muttered something about 'useful exposure'.

'So how to put Gippsworld on the star-chart?' asked the President, tapping his nose in a conspiratorial way. The film flickered on, and this time a slide flashed up above the room which read 'WHERE NEXT FOR GIPPSWORLD?'

'The solution, my friends, is *tourism*. It's going to be our number one new growth industry.'

A couple of the audience stuck their hands up. 'But why would anybody want to come *here*?' said Misha, a young pig farmer with a pleasant, open face. There was some general nodding. Even the methane farmers agreed that this seemed like a salient point.

7

'A very good question,' said the President. 'And that's exactly why I called this meeting. I thought we could have a collective brainstorm. Throw a few ideas at the wall, see what sticks.'

Another slide shimmered overhead. This one said 'IDEAS'.

'So, who wants to go first?'

It took a while for anybody to volunteer, because Gippsworld was a taciturn place and few of the inhabitants fancied themselves as public speakers, but eventually Yuri, who was in charge of keeping the plasma generators clean, cleared his throat.

'Over the years quite a few depressed locals have killed themselves by jumping into our famous never-completed mineshaft,' he said. 'So perhaps we could encourage tourists to come here to do the same. Establish ourselves as a suicide hot-spot. Set up a stall, sell them farewell knick-knacks.' There was a good deal of excited chatter about this, until someone pointed out that 'farewell knick-knacks' weren't really a thing. Probably there was a boring moral question as well, but the real clincher, Misha argued, was that a half-dug hole on an out-of-the-way rock, even if it had briefly been a *celebrated* hole seventy years ago, wasn't going to be able to compete with the galaxy's more glamorous suicide hotspots. Nobody was likely to jump down a mineshaft when they could vaporise themselves crashing a rented starship into the rings of Isis Nine, or burn their faces off diving from the thousand-mile span of the Sapphire Bridge into the magma lakes of Cassiopeia.

And so they moved on.

A couple of the more unbalanced citizens thought it would be good to commit some sort of atrocity. Planets where atrocities had happened, they reasoned, always got crazy amounts of tourists. But nobody could agree on what

8

kind of atrocity would be best. The pig farmers suggested some kind of mysterious mass murder where all the methane farmers were – regrettably – found dead in their beds. The methane farmers were in favour of the planet having a brief, unfortunate flirtation with fascism leading to all the pig farmers being hung from lampposts.

Since that discussion didn't seem to be going anywhere, someone else suggested they could try to pretend the mine-shaft was haunted, maybe dress it up with a skeleton or two. They already had quite a few spare skeletons from the aforementioned suicides. A haunted mineshaft seemed like a decent draw, but this time nobody could agree on the best kind of haunting. Unimaginative opinion was split between 'inevitable ghostly child wreaking revenge for bullying' and 'predictable eldritch curse from building on a hitherto unknown civilisation's dumb sacred burial ground'. So that idea got put on the back-burner as well.

Dmitry, the air traffic supervisor, proposed they could become famous for being the planet with the Most Beautiful Woman In The Galaxy. But everyone knew that *that* was just Dmitry's way of trying to flirt with Olga, the co-air traffic supervisor, and also that a) Olga wasn't interested in Dmitry, and b) she couldn't really pass for the most beautiful woman in the Galaxy, even though she was perfectly fine looking, because she had that weird thing she did with her eyebrows.

Finally, somebody suggested they could 'have a parade' on the grounds that 'people like parades'. Somebody else declared that the worst idea yet. The person whose idea it had been said that kind of criticism wasn't in the spirit of brain-storming, then the other person told him what he could do with his brainstorming and his blue-sky-thinking whilst he was at it, and before long the population of Gippsworld were having a brawl and smacking each other

9

with sticks and it didn't matter how many times the President banged his gavel and so the meeting was adjourned.

* * *

The hover-truck skimmed back through town towards the Bulgakovs' pig farm.

'I think the President made some very good points,' said Misha, gazing out of a rain-streaked window as they sped past the rotting foundations of the Olympic-sized velodrome and the vacant lot where the opera house would have gone. His father snorted.

'He is idiot dreamer,' said Misha Senior.

'What about the graph? That graph seemed pretty convincing.'

'Graphs are for methane farmers and simpletons.'

Misha watched as the unfinished city gave way to claggy, monochrome fields of mud. 'I've been saying for ages that we should consider branching out from pigs,' he persisted. 'We could do a part-exchange on the *Malkovich*, get something a bit nippier, a bit more space-worthy, do some proper long-haul trading. You know: in commodities that people actually want to buy. Commodities that don't make them throw up all the time. You could take it easy down here. Kick back, learn space golf or something.'

'Putin give me strength. This is one of your "projects".'

'I've given it a lot of thought.'

'You mean you design logo for company.'

'I've not *just* designed a logo,' said Misha. 'I did a tagline too. *Bulgakov Trading – Outstanding in our Field*. Next to a picture of us on our farm. Farm/fields. It's a play on words, you see?'

Misha Senior went on staring at the road ahead. 'Your great-grandfather farm pigs. Your grandfather farm pigs. I farm pigs. You farm pigs. Though mostly you do not farm pigs. Mostly you sit on fleshy arse, eating my cereal.'

'You're not seeing the big picture! You need more *vision*, dad. What's so great about pig farming anyway?'

'Pig farming is hard life. Second highest number of industrial accidents after mining. Good, honest work.'

Misha rolled his eyes.

'It's not like they're even pigs,' he muttered.

The pigs were not *technically* pigs. So far as anyone could tell, they were ambulatory plants, brainless, bone-free, stump-legged Triffids. A few passing botanists had theorised that the fact Gippsworld's dominant life form relied on photosynthesis indicated the planet's weather had, in some distant past, been less unremittingly dismal. For millennia the plant-pigs had been locked in an arms race with the sky, getting more and more efficient at extracting energy from whatever watery sunlight made it through the remorseless cloud cover, like drunks magically locating the alcohol in a bathroom cabinet. Now, if you shone a bright enough light source at their hyper-black skin they'd overdo it and explode in a gloopy shower of vegetable matter. On otherwise boring evenings, kids would sneak into the farm and try to blow the pigs up with a torch for a joke. It was the sort of fact that made it into the light-hearted 'and finally' column of a few nature journals, but no academic could be bothered to do much fieldwork on a place like Gippsworld, so that was as far as studies had gone.

'Always you are coming up with these schemes,' said Misha Senior. 'It is same as when you said you would be comics artist. Or when you were going to be zoo keeper. Or when you were going to be in band.'

'The band was really good. It's hard to get decent representation these days.'

'You had four omnichord players. No drummer even.' His father shook his head sadly. 'Awful, awful sound.'

'I just think the President is right,' said Misha. 'We need to move with the times. In his book on *Innovating The Workplace Via Space-War*, Cliff Ganymede says a business, like a shark, must constantly swim forward, or it will be eaten by a moon whale or a squid.'

'Oooff. Again with Cliff Ganymede. Always his stories filling your head with tales of exciting adventure beyond the stars. I know what it is. You feel destined for some life greater than pig farming. A life much more exotic, yes? Well. There is reason for this.'

Misha Senior pulled the hover-truck over to the side of the road and rested his chin on the wheel. He exhaled a heavy, whistling sigh.

'There is something I must tell you.' The old man sounded tired and resigned. 'I think maybe you have long suspected it. The truth is …' He paused for a moment. 'I am not your actual father, Misha. Your real father was great hero. An Elite space ace. He fought brave secret battle in the Alioth Rebellion of 3228. When he was dying, I swore to him I would raise you as my own, out of harm's way, but now I see: is pointless to try to fight the destiny that courses through your blood.'

'What?' Misha's mouth opened and closed like the door of a broken elevator, except up and down, not sideways. 'What?' he said again.

'Oh, sweet mother of Belka and Strelka. Look at your stupid plate face.' Misha Senior cuffed his son round the ear. 'You want to know why *really* you feel destined for great things? Because you are idiot dreamer just like President. All so many dreams, but no follow-through. Wasting money on expensive notebooks to write big ideas down.'

12

Misha scowled. He knew that using *paper* notebooks in the thirty-fourth century was a pretty daft affectation, but he'd seen a show where at the start of each episode Cliff Ganymede, sat behind his sturdy non-synthetic desk, introduced the upcoming space adventure with a real leather-bound journal in his hands. And Misha really liked Cliff Ganymede.

'Nice stationery is important for the creative process,' he mumbled.

'You never even fill up notebook! I know this because I found one. You write "sit-ups x 100". You write "learn coding language". Then five pages of drawings of girls in tight tops. You want to know something?'

'Not really.'

'You are much better at drawing boobs than faces. Also, you have no perseverance. You say you will do a thing, then you waste time playing Cliff Ganymede computer game. How are you going be daring intergalactic space-trader when you are never even getting around to doing ship's health and safety check?'

Misha Senior started the truck up again and it bobbed on down the road.

'By the way, who is "Phoebe"?'

'Phoebe …?' Misha pretended to try to recall a Phoebe. 'I think *maybe* there's a Phoebe works up on the space station. I don't remember exactly. Why do you ask?'

'Along with the sketches of girls and ideas for terrible films, you have written down the name Phoebe many times. Sometimes you have drawn flowers next to it.' Misha Senior shook his head pityingly. 'Is good your mother is dead in violent threshing machine accident to not see this type of thing.'

* * *

Back at the farm, Misha lay on his bunk and called up his copy of *Are You A Man Or A Thargoid? – Taking Control Of Your Life The Cliff Ganymede Way*. He zoomed through to a random chapter and started to read.

It's the easiest thing in the world to give up. I could have given up in episode ten of 'Galloping Ganymede!' when I found myself trapped in that asteroid field, a battalion of Thargoids breathing their foul insect breath down my neck. But I did not. I lasered their stupid Thargoid faces in. And by following my Eight Steps To Willpower, you will too! Obviously, because of the current uneasy peace, the Thargoids in your case will be metaphorical Thargoids, but whether it's preparing for those accountancy exams or impressing a date, the principle still stands. There is an Old Earth expression I like – Carpe diem! It translates as 'Don't delay, seize that fish before it rots!'

Misha switched the book off again and with a resolute firmness of purpose that he was sure would make Cliff Ganymede proud flicked on his personal subspace interface and called up Officer Phoebe Clag's dating profile.

He started to type.

```
Hello. We've never spoken, but I keep noticing
you around the docking bays when I've been
passing through. I have often watched you
issuing spot-fines or checking cargo manifests
and hoped that someday you might check mine.
Does that make me sound like a stalker? I'm
not! I don't want to dress up in a suit fash-
ioned from your skin or anything terrible like
that. You do have lovely skin though — it
would make for a great skin-suit if I WAS
crazy!
```

14

He read it back, shook his head in horror, and tried once more.

```
Hello to you, Ms Clag. I happened across your
profile, and note that you are interested in
meeting new people, as I am myself. A bit
about me: I enjoy many kinds of music, unusual
wines, laughing with friends, and have read
all of Cliff Ganymede's self-improvement books.
I also consider myself a cineaste.
```

He clenched his teeth and hit delete.

```
Hi! Maybe it would be neat to hang out some
time? In fact — officer — I think it would
be a CRIME not to!!!
```

'Oh god,' whispered Misha under his breath. 'Oh *good god*.' He started again.

```
Hey there. Wasn't it the ancient philosopher
Melvyn Bragg who said…
```

Two hours later – after deleting a draft which began *'Whoop! Is that the sound of the police?'* and then went on to feature an elaborate ASCII picture of a plant-pig doing a thumbs up – Misha logged out. He sighed, reached under his pillow, pulled out his notebook, the one with 'LET'S HAVE AN INNOVATION JAM' printed on the cover, flipped to the page marked *Misha's Achievement List*, and found where he'd written the word 'Phoebe'. He carefully wrote the words 'STILL PENDING' next to it. The item after 'Phoebe' was 'Malkovich – Important Health & Safety Check.' He would

15

do that right now because regardless of what his dad said he was a dynamic and proactive individual. He looked at the clock in the corner of his retina-overlay: Three minutes past nine. It might be an idea, Misha reasoned proactively, to start work *on the hour*, with a nice round number. That would be a cleaner mental space. He flipped on the entertainment channel. It was enough time for one quick game of Cliff Ganymede's *Mission: Thargoid Kill-Punch.*

When Misha next noticed the clock he saw it had somehow crept to ten past ten, so, still keen to start work exactly on the hour, he decided to go on playing for a little while longer. Thirty minutes later he dutifully logged off, and went to make a thermos of coffee. Then he got side-tracked into staring out of the kitchen window for a while. Once he'd stopped doing that he realised it was now six minutes past eleven, which kind of messed up his plans. If he was going to start work on the hour he'd have to wait until midnight. Better, perhaps, to write it off as a bad job for this evening and punch some more Thargoids. Get it out of his system. That way he could wake up early tomorrow, do the health and safety check, and then, with the wind in his sails, he would be bound to have a really productive day. He resolved to put the new deadline in his notebook. He would use extra heavy lettering, and underline it twice. And this time he would definitely, finally, send his message to Phoebe Clag.

Chapter Two

Construction had started on the space station *Jim Bergerac* a few months before Gippsworld's rich natural resources turned out to be worth bupkis, so half of it was what *Architectural Exercises In Narcissism*'s presenter would term 'radical froufrou', with mock Greek columns in the corridors and coolant pipes that didn't drip everywhere and nice scatter cushions, and half of it was built out of paste and packing crates and chunks of old satellites mashed together with whatever other space flotsam had come to hand. In the shabbier section of the huge creaking doughnut, under a dirty plexiglass dome, a young police officer ate some synthetic noodles out of a pot.

The best thing about the *Jim Bergerac*'s observation deck, in Phoebe's opinion, was that the view was poor. Nobody ever stopped by to marvel at the unimposing grey lump that was Gippsworld spinning away in the void, or at the ugly, floating black rectangle that was the planet's unused advertising hoarding. This meant she could spend her entire lunch break stretched out on a row of seats undisturbed, and watch the rolling news blather away across the display beamed out from the pea-sized projector implanted in her eyebrow. The headline had been the same all afternoon.

CLIFF GANYMEDE:
AUTHOR, ACTOR, GURU, BELOVED BY MILLIONS
– MURDERED!

- Life-coach Cliff Ganymede, 112, found dead in his hotel room.
- 'I'll miss his elaborate beehive metaphors the most,' says agent who found body.
- Our hardworking boys and girls in blue chasing up leads.

Concern grew for Ganymede after he failed to turn up for the latest leg of a nine-planet book tour, scheduled to promote his new self-help manual, The Only Thing Stopping You Is You, And Those Thargoid Bastards.

Ganymede first rose to prominence with his hard-to-categorise, semi-autobiographical novels – a unique blend of high adventure, flow-charts, graphic sex and motivational life-tips. How I Fought Off The Swamp Mandrills Of Turlough Twelve And Simultaneously Learned To Choose Myself, Six Effective Social Media Habits That Helped Me Explode The Imperial Ambassador, *and* Assault On Arcturus: Preparing My CV *were among his many early hits. He later diversified into both television and games, with equal success.* Mission: Thargoid Kill-Punch *has sold over half a billion copies and is estimated to have inspired at least that same number of tedious opinion columns.*

Cliff's prose style was variously described by critics as 'magnetic, but with the same polarity as eyeballs, and therefore incredibly difficult to read', 'challenging', and 'leaving you with a sensation akin to trying to breathe meringue'. His acting – he played 'Clive Ganymede', a thinly fictionalised version of himself for sixty seasons of the hit show Galloping Ganymede! *– came in for even harsher criticism. 'Though the role of "Clive" might not be considered a stretch for Commander Ganymede,' wrote the Alioth Nova, 'he still seems to deliver his lines as though discovering language for the very first time.' But despite these brickbats from the press, Ganymede was never less than wildly popular with the general public, consistently voted number one in the* Middlebrow Chat! Magazine ManBooker *awards.*

The investigation into his murder is ongoing.

It was exactly the kind of exciting and mysterious case that Phoebe had gone through six years of police academy to work on. Dogged detective work required. A high pressure, high-profile assignment carried out under the glare of the media spotlight. But Phoebe didn't work in homicide. Phoebe worked in the customs and excise unit of a police force who had jurisdiction over a solar system that contained a level of illicit trading activity so close to *nil* as to be Statistically Irrelevant, according to the latest crime census.

She scratched her stomach, and thought about poor life decisions.

She wondered if she should wash the synthi-noodle stain out of her top.

She wondered how much synthi-noodle she must have eaten to stain a Teflon-weave, StayClean police shirt in the first place.

She wondered what the chances had been of this new stain combining with the old stain to create what now looked like an angry face.

She wondered if she had maybe let her personal hygiene standards slip a little.

She wondered if there was a record for the amount of synthi-noodle consumed in a single afternoon.

'What a bowl of cocks,' she said out loud, to nobody.

Lunch had officially ended five minutes ago. She should be back on her beat, carrying out the random cargo spot-checks that made up the bulk of her dreary, pointless days. But she knew in advance how that would go: she'd either patrol the docking bays on foot or pootle about near-space in the Police Viper for a few hours, and if she was lucky some dreary, pointless methane shipment might head out in her general direction. She'd stop it, go aboard, there'd be a bit of forcibly sunny small talk. They'd probably make a dreary, pointless remark about her cybernetic leg. She'd do a semi-comprehensive check depending on how lazy she was feeling and find exactly zero contraband. Maybe a few smuggled episodes of *Laser, Baby & C.H.O.M.P.S.* or *Neil's Nine* if they happened to be heading past Placet B. None of it would be worth the energy or effort, and she'd have another stack of admin to hide somewhere. 'Most Likely To Do A Thorough And Conscientious Job' it had said under her yearbook picture. Perhaps, thought Phoebe, she should spend the afternoon looking at videos of sloths falling asleep in zero gravity.

The *blip* of a call coming in over the network interrupted her wallow, and she guiltily hit answer before she had a chance to register that it wasn't anything to do with work – it was her mother.

'How are you doing, flower?' Her mother's big floating head popped into a space a few inches from her face, automatically and nightmarishly keeping pace with any eyeball movement, because Phoebe had forgotten to turn that setting off. 'Is everything all right? I'm not interrupting?'

'Hi, kind of, things are pretty busy here.'

'I can imagine! I saw the news. Are you working the Cliff Ganymede case?'

'No mother, I've explained this before, that's not the sort of policing I do.'

'You used to love mysteries and murders and things. I remember how you drew that darling picture of a bleeding skull when you were only a toddler. With the maggots! We all thought you'd become an artist.'

'Mother, I've—'

But Mrs Clag was already up and running into an account

20

of the goings-on back on Gurney Slade Six. Phoebe drifted off during a detailed anecdote about the new model of food printer her father had installed and the type of warranty that came with it. In the distance a couple of Phoebe's colleagues patrolled the nothingness. Gippsworld went on not looking anything like a blue jewel. Phoebe only zoned back in when she realised she was being asked a question.

'Don't you think, petal?'

'Sorry, what?'

'That you should try to get out and socialise more. You know you have a tendency to bury yourself away.'

There was a meaningful pause.

'Have you met anybody?'

At this inevitable point in the call, Phoebe squirmed and rolled her eyes, causing her mother's head to do a juddering loop-the-loop.

'No, mother. Like I said, I've been busy. Work things.'

'Do you ever hear from Glen? We really liked Glen.'

'Glen,' said Phoebe, as firmly as she could manage, 'was a twat.'

'But such lovely cheekbones. And those teeth! Anyhow, that's not relevant, because your father and I wanted you to know that you absolutely shouldn't feel any pressure on the relationship front. Neither of us are the *slightest* bit worried about that. The Kewleys next door, did you know their Janey didn't have a kid until she was *seventy*? It's amazing what they can do these days. Besides, you can grow babies in jars. Sometimes the face comes out a bit wonky, like Megan at number fifteen, but mostly you can't even tell. Not that there's any reason you should feel you ought to procreate anyhow. We just want you to be *happy*.'

There were only so many relentlessly upbeat assurances

21

that her life wasn't a crushing disappointment that Phoebe could take in a day, so after another couple of minutes she pretended a klaxon was going off.

'Sorry mum,' she said, waving. 'The thin blue line never sleeps!'

'Okay dear, we miss you—' The words died on Mrs Clag's holographic lips as she vanished into the sub-ether. Phoebe breathed deeply, thought about sitting up, but decided she wasn't in a rush. She checked her inbox.

```
Your CosmicSexMingle profile has been viewed
one hundred and eighteen (118) times this week
by User FinePigs21. You have zero (0) messages
from User FinePigs21.
```

She scrolled on.

```
Alicia Breen wants to reconnect on CopLink!
The professional network for the police force
of the Foster System. Message from Alicia:
'Ciao bella! Would love to catch up. Seems a
thousand years since the academy! Guess what?
I've been assigned to the Cliff Ganymede case—'
```

Phoebe quickly flicked it over to the trash. She tried to think calming thoughts about dogs with sad eyes.

She wondered why anyone would batter the system's biggest, most popular star to death with a hardback copy of his best-selling sex-and-spreadsheets manual *Be A Gas Giant In The Boardroom & The Bedroom, Not A Nebula*.

She wondered why, as his final act, Ganymede had scrawled the words 'knuckle down' across the title page in his own blood.

She wondered whether that bonehead Alicia still had a mouth that looked like a paper-cut.

She should stop dwelling on it. She should stop thinking about unsolved murders and think about tax evasion and export licences instead. Be constructive with her time. Concentrate on her job. Maybe, if she concentrated hard enough, something interesting might turn up. She rubbed the label on her empty pot of noodles.

'What's the largest amount of synthi-noodle consumed by a human being in a single afternoon?' she asked the interactive packaging.

'Fifty pots!' replied Chet Noodles, the relentlessly chirpy, anthropomorphic embodiment of the SynNoodle brand, dancing across the label. 'Set by Nils-Olof Franzen, deceased, on Lansbury Five. Synthetic noodle RDA is zero pots.'

She flopped out an arm and waved for a baristabot.

'Hit me,' said Phoebe. She was going for the record.

Chapter Three

Anyone landing on Gippsworld who wasn't drunk or lost or trying to sell encyclopaedias would have caused a stir, but the stranger who turned up at the spaceport that morning left an actual audible thrum of excitement in his wake. The ship he climbed out from was sleek and expensive-looking and had jazzy blue zigzags down the side. The man himself was even more sleek and expensive-looking. He wore a glittering, phosphorescent cravat and an old-fashioned, white Zirconium suit. It looked handmade rather than printed. Misha had never seen a handmade suit before. He'd also never seen such a daringly pointless little beard, or such a thrillingly asymmetrical haircut. He'd been hosing down the pig transport when the stranger doffed his hat at him. Not having a hat to doff himself, he waggled his hose awkwardly in reply, because he didn't know what else to do.

When the stranger stopped off at the spaceport's greasy bar and grill, Rita Korolev, who always had a tendency to start drinking early, reported breathlessly that he'd ordered a type of coffee none of the baristabots had ever heard of. And as he then proceeded to wander the streets, past the now-mostly-crumbling local architecture, the wave of gossip swelled. He kept stopping and taking pictures of things that didn't look as if they needed to have their pictures taken: broken masonry, abandoned plasma silos, dead birds. When the locals, pretending they just happened to be out for a stroll or had dropped something in his vicinity, sidled up as close as they dared, they'd noticed him muttering into his sleeve. Someone reported hearing the phrase 'unique cultural mindset'. Somebody else was sure he'd also said 'rich tapestry'. It was confusing. Usually when an off-worlder accidentally landed on Gippsworld they stuck to phrases like *'Jesus Christ'* and *'I swear to god, Gavin, if you don't fix that navigation unit I'm taking the kids and moving back to Phobos'*.

Occasionally, the man would stop and ask people something about their lives, but then, instead of rolling his eyes and yawning at the inevitable boring pig- or methane-based anecdote – like a normal person would – he'd say, *"Fascinating!"* and compliment them on their unspoilt, earthy charm.

One of the methane farm girls said that she'd heard he was an anthropologist. Another said that they'd heard a rumour he was something big in marketing. Rita claimed she had it on good authority that he was a high-powered mineral trader. From one of the core worlds. Maybe the *empire*, even. Certainly somewhere very cosmopolitan, *you can just tell from his bearing*, she added, knowledgeably.

The thing that really got everyone worked up was what happened when the stranger bumped into Mad Vladimir, the city's resident hobo. Mad Vladimir, as usual, was seated outside the never-completed fifth-deepest mine in the galaxy, next to a trestle table piled high with his weird, shapeless sculptures. These were things he made out of Gippsworld's thick, grey, ubiquitous mud. Nobody knew what they were meant to be. Occasionally, someone would speculate that one looked a bit like a golem, or an ant, or possibly a figurative representation of despair. But if they asked Mad Vladimir what it was he'd just bark or grunt and ask for some vodka.

This didn't seem to put the stranger off at all. When he saw the pile of sculptures, he almost bounced up and down with excitement.

'These are astounding,' proclaimed the stranger, seizing one of the lumpier efforts and holding it reverentially up to the light as if it was some sort of relic. 'The genuine article.' Then he said a lot more stuff about 'pure primitive lines' and the 'searing truth of the untrained hand'. He asked Mad Vladimir if his art was for sale. Mad Vladimir grunted. Not to be deterred, the stranger pulled out a pile of pre-loaded credits, and pressed them into Vladimir's hand.

'There you go,' he said, loud enough for all the eaves-dropping locals who were still loitering about nearby to hear. 'Ten credits for the lot. And I'll return tomorrow to purchase any more that you happen to have produced.'

A few Gippsworldians argued that the stranger must be nuts. Rita, whom people were starting to find kind of irri-tating, said that in fact she'd long been a fan of Vladimir's work, and was surprised that it had gone unappreciated for all this while. There was some debate about whether they should start referring to Mad Vladimir as Affluent Vladimir now. More than a couple of the locals reasoned that if Affluent Vladimir, a certified bum, could produce sculptures that lunatic off-worlders wanted to buy, then how hard could this art lark be?

As promised, the next day the man in the white suit returned, only to find, now waiting for him along with Vladimir, another half dozen Gippsworldians who had discovered hitherto unseen outsider art skills, their various pots and sculptures piled high on more tables. Without missing a beat, the stranger surveyed these new artworks, proclaimed them good, and purchased them all on the spot, for even more than he'd paid before. This time, before disappearing back to his ship, he hung up a little sign by the entrance to the mineshaft:

Genuine indigenous outsider art sought.
Sculptures, pottery, misc. artefacts, etc.
Top prices paid.
Will return each day.

Gippsworld went crazy.

* * *

'This once sleepy backwater is abuzz—'
  '… it's a new sensation shaking up the art establishment—'
  '… sure to be this year's must-have gift—'
  '… Cliff Ganymede murder, still unsolved, almost forgotten about in all this hubbub—'

Misha kept flicking through the newsfeeds, but they were all full of the same excited babble they'd been plastered with for weeks. Mud sculpture this. Mud sculpture that. In the space of a month just about everybody on Gippsworld had forgotten about pigs and methane altogether and set themselves up as Indigenous Artists. The stranger had kept coming back – every afternoon without fail – buying up sculptures by the skip-load. Before long he was joined by other strangers, who did the same. Then the news crews had turned up. Soon there were lots of charts with arrows pointing upwards and serious jowly-necked experts explaining that they'd always suspected this exact thing might happen.

Misha stopped on one of the channels for a moment. His neighbour Nikolai was being interviewed by a skinny woman who seemed to enjoy nodding. It took Misha a moment to recognise Nikolai, because instead of the usual filthy coveralls he wore to unblock the New Vladimir-Putingrad silage gullies, he now had a pipe in his mouth and was wearing a billowy sort of smock. According to the caption on the picture he was 'At the forefront of the Gippsworld Outsider Art Movement'.

'*Well, the thing is, Diane,*' Nikolai was saying to the reporter, '*it's not about the subject per se, it's about recontextualising the imagery associated with that subject.*'

'*Which is why your work, Horse 1, doesn't actually look like a horse?*'

'*Exactly.*'

'*So tell me, Nicky. Your overnight artistic success has led to you becoming, along with many other residents of New Vladimir-Putingrad, incredibly rich. Have you got any plans as to how you're going to spend that money?*'

'*Diane, an artist like me isn't really interested in the vulgar products of the military-industrial complex, but I thought I might buy a yacht and a platinum hat.*'

Misha flicked again. An academic with unruly eyebrows was in the middle of explaining how the Gippsworld outsider art movement was *authentic* because the Gippsworldians were more naturally attuned to nature than inhabitants of other, more developed planets. Misha scratched his head. He vaguely remembered Nikolai getting arrested for trying to do something nobody liked to talk about to one of the pig-plants the previous winter. He guessed that counted as being attuned to nature.

'Are you watching your programs all day,' said Misha's father, sticking his head round the door, 'or are you going to get off spherical lazy arse and do works? These pigs do not harvest themselves.'

* * *

28

'So, I was thinking,' said Misha, as he and his father waded out into the boggy field and started to round up the latest pig crop, 'that I might try my hand at a bit of this sculpture making. It really seems to have caught on.'

'We had this conversation. No more schemes.'

'It's not a "scheme". And it's actually kind of crazy not to. Literally everybody is doing it. You know Sergey?'

'Latvian-faced Sergey?'

'Yes, Latvian-faced Sergey. His last piece went for nineteen credits. NINETEEN. That's more than our truck cost.'

'Is fad.' Misha's father made a dismissive snorting noise, and went on prodding livestock out of the curdling mud, up a ramp and into a cargo container, which bobbed around in an ungainly way as it hovered on a cushion of dirty air a couple of feet above the ground. 'We are proud pig people.'

'We had a leaflet through the door just yesterday offering to take the farm off our hands.'

'Yes, I saw. To turn into parking lot. Why do we need new parking lot?'

'Because the economy is booming! You know, even the Melnikovs sold up.' Misha shook his head sadly. 'They've opened a gallery space. It has its own juice-bar. Soon we'll be the only ones left in pigs.'

'Good, less competition. We'll have cornered the market.'

'We'll have cornered the market in a product nobody wants.'

Misha sulkily used his plasma-lasso to yank one of the plant-pigs, straggling away from the herd, back into line. 'Besides. I think I'd have a natural flair for it.'

'You say this because you have womanish hands, like a methane farmer. You are oddly proud of these womanish hands of yours.'

'There's nothing wrong with having some *ambition*, dad. Think what we could do with the money. Even you must occasionally *covet* something.'

Misha Senior paused for a moment, and stroked his beard. After a while he said, 'I would like to have lunch with Zargella Lombard.'

'The movie star?'

'She has fine, broad hips. Free from childhood disease, I think.'

'Okay, sure, but, I mean, apart from that?'

'Hush, Misha. The wittering is making me tired.'

As the last of the plant-pigs snorted and shuffled into the floating box, Misha's father banged the door shut and bolted it with a firm *clang* that also signified the end of any conversation.

'No son of mine makes pottery knick-knacks. There is no future in this.' He handed Misha the keys to the hover truck.

'You take pigs to space station. Sell pigs. Do not moon over the girls.'

* * *

Gippsworld's spaceport, like everywhere else on Gippsworld, was starting to go up in the world. It still looked like a toilet, but a bit of effort had gone into making everything slightly less bleak. The windows on the control tower had been cleaned for the first time in years. A banner above the arrivals lounge, which previously had just displayed a contact number for the Galactic Samaritans, now wished arrivals a happy stay and pointed towards the array of new art galleries and an artisanal bakery.

Misha finished transferring sixty recalcitrant plant-pigs from the shipping container into the big square bulk of the

Malkovich's cargo hold and punched a few details into the automatic air traffic control unit. It bleeped at him, letting him know that a take-off slot wouldn't be ready for another hour. Misha swore and puffed out his cheeks. A month ago he wouldn't have had to wait at all. But where once the departure gates had been empty except for the odd broken-down shuttle bus, now he counted at least a dozen shimmering out-of-town ships. Some of them looked as if they'd come from a really long way away. Actual proper space traders with thousand-yard stares and the hunched shoulders that resulted from a hard life of interminable hyperspace jumps loitered around, looking surly. Misha wanted to talk to them. He wanted to ask if they'd ever seen a supernova, or a building with more than three storeys, or if it was true that on some planets there was enough sunlight for men and women to wander around with no tops on. But he didn't dare, so instead he just satisfied himself with ticking off a Lakon Spaceways Type 6 Transporter and a Core Dynamics Python in his *Gollancz Bumper Book Of Space Going Vessels*, and decided to get some lunch at the café whilst he waited.

* * *

'Up a bit. No, it's still not straight.'

The President was standing by the spaceport café entrance supervising two baristabots who were in the process of hanging a painting above the sandwich bar. The painting, a lurid triptych, showed the President wrestling with a Jovian moontiger, an eagle and a mule.

'Misha, isn't it?' said the President, spinning around as Misha came in through the door. The President was good with names, which was half the reason he was president.

'Take five, guys,' he said, clicking his fingers at the bots. He beamed. 'Mind if I sit with you?' he asked, already sliding into the booth opposite Misha. 'Word of advice, don't have the eggs.'

Misha picked up a menu, and nodded appreciatively at the painting. 'You've wrestled a lot of creatures, Mister President.'

'Oh, well, you know,' the President waved away the compliment, even though he was obviously pleased the subject had come up. 'Some of them are a bit exaggerated. But it's important to maintain a dynamic image. I find pictures of me wrestling creatures whilst shirtless is one of the best ways to communicate that. Lesson one from Putin's classic work on political leadership. Putin was a famous old-world Russian dictator. One of my historical heroes.'

'Oh yes, we did him at school. And he gets a few mentions in Cliff Ganymede's book on *Getting Your Message Across – What I learnt About PR from Mass Thargoid Genocide.*' Misha studied the picture a bit more closely. 'Did eagles really used to have two heads?'

'Apparently the old Russian ones did,' the President said with a shrug.

'I wonder how it ate? What if the heads had a difference of opinion? What if one head wanted worms and the other head wanted mouse guts?'

'I don't know, Misha – it's a very interesting point you raise.' The President suddenly leaned forward, and pulled a hopeful expression. 'Speaking of raising interesting points, and of differences of opinion, did you have that talk with your dad?'

'Yeah. He's still pretty committed to the pig trading business.'

There was a long, difficult pause. The President's face clouded over. 'That's a shame,' he said. 'That's a very great shame indeed.'

'He's a stubborn old bastard,' agreed Misha.

'The truth is,' said the President, reaching across the table and putting his hand on Misha's shoulder like a creepy, friendly uncle, 'I just want the best for all my subjects. Voters. Whatever the technical term is. I don't like the thought of you missing this golden opportunity.'

Misha nodded. 'Things do seem to be taking off round here.'

'Exactly! It's a bold, bright new future. Just between you and me, there's talk of finally finishing the municipal centre roof. Who knows, one day we might even be able to switch the giant billboard on. This whole art thing has really turned our fortunes around. Did you hear that we've actually had to bring in off-worlders to start doing the jobs people can't be bothered to do anymore? It's expensive, but that's okay, because everyone's a lot richer now. Well, almost everyone.' He said that last bit with a pointed look.

Misha glumly typed his order into the booth's printer. An unappetising tuna melt sprayed onto his plate.

'We need all the indigenous artists we can get our hands on,' the President continued. 'In fact, at the current rate we'll have to set up factories to deal with the order backlog. Gippsworld is going places! And *you* should be going places too.'

'I'll keep working on him, but don't hold your breath,' said Misha, taking a resigned bite of his sandwich. 'It took me five years to convince him that filtering the brainworms out of our water supply wasn't a "ridiculous bourgeois affectation".'

Misha finished his food, which the President insisted on paying for, and apologised again. Then he wandered back

33

to where the *Malkovich* was parked, and climbed up into the boxy cockpit. He whistled a melancholy little tune as he waited for the light that would indicate his take-off slot had cleared. It eventually flashed green, and he clicked the ignition. The jets roared beneath him. Even though he was flying what was technically categorised as a barn, the g-force was briefly thrilling. The ship rattled and shook its way upwards, through the clouds and the drizzle, past the stupid billboard, and finally burst out through the top of the miserable troposphere and into the shining blackness of outer space. For a few moments, for the not-quite-twenty minute journey between the spaceport and the nearby *Jim Bergerac*, Misha could pretend that, much like Cliff Ganymede, he was blasting off towards an exciting adventure. Encounters with pirates, assassins and girls wearing impractical space-leotards.

A thick, bubbling, popping sound brought him back to the moment. Misha unstrapped himself, stepped into his magno-boots, and went to check the cargo. He had left a light on in the hold. One of the pigs, having drifted a bit too close to it, had over-photosynthesised. Misha groaned, picked up a vacuum cleaner, and opened the door. Pig bits floated out and lodged in his hair.

I am, thought Misha with a sigh, *some way off from meeting girls dressed in impractical space-leotards.*

Chapter Four

Phoebe, excited for the first time in months, waited on the bench outside Detective Sergeant Peterson's office and jiggled her cybernetic leg. It didn't seem to be adjusting very well to the *Jim Bergerac*'s flaky pressure changes lately, and she really wanted to fiddle about with the settings, but that would have meant opening the squeaky hatch on her shin and she was already feeling self-conscious enough. On the noticeboard opposite some clever dick had scrawled a crude figure of a stick-woman, readily identifiable because of an explanatory arrow with 'Phoebe, the Mechanical Lady' written next to it. The stick-woman was kissing a refrigeration unit, and a speech bubble coming out of her mouth said 'OH MISTER REFRIGERATOR I WANT TO SEX YOU'. Phoebe's colleagues did not score highly on their workplace discrimination courses.

Something buzzed, and a plastic receptionist cheerfully informed Phoebe that Sergeant Peterson was free to see her now.

'Officer Clag! What's afoot?' Peterson beamed at her from behind his desk like a benign corpulent bear. That was always his greeting. 'What's afoot?' When she had first heard it, Phoebe assumed Peterson was having a go at her leg, but soon discovered he was simply being arch. The assumption being: things were never afoot in the vicinity of the *Jim Bergerac*.

She tried to sound professional and business-like but couldn't keep the note of excitement out of her voice. 'Well, sir,' she said, marvelling as usual at just how rectangular his blocky, ursine head was, 'I think something strange is going on. Something *interesting*.'

'Really?' Peterson looked understandably doubtful. He stroked his moustache in an unconvinced sort of way.

'There have been anomalies.'

'Anomalies?'

'Anomalies.' Phoebe fought back a grin. 'As you know, with the recent unexpected boom in the Gippsworld art market, we've been having quite a few more traders turn up in the system.'

'Yes, haven't seen the place so busy in years. Exciting times! I was thinking of getting one myself – a sculpture, that is – as a conversation piece for the dining room. Mrs Peterson is terribly keen.'

Phoebe nodded, and tried to keep her boss on track. 'Well, here's the interesting bit. I've done fifty-nine spot-checks in the past couple of weeks, and in thirty of those, do you know what I found?' She paused dramatically.

'Go on.'

'*Nothing*.'

'Ah,' Peterson frowned, seemingly non-plussed.

'Nothing at all. By which I mean the ships *weren't carrying the cargo they said they were*. They had "Gippsworld indigenous peoples' artwork" listed on the manifest, but nothing in the hold.'

'Oh.'

It wasn't quite the reaction she'd hoped for. 'I mean to say, that's odd, isn't it?' she persisted. 'Especially given that they'd already paid the shipping tax.'

'Is it a crime, though? Not carrying things? It doesn't

sound like much of a crime,' Peterson looked deep in thought for a moment, and patted his pockets. 'I'm not carrying anything right now. I often don't.'

'Well, no, I suppose when you look at it that way ...' Phoebe floundered and did her best to grab on to why it had all seemed so important ten minutes ago. 'But it's puzzling.'

'And what did the traders say when you asked about this "anomaly"?'

'Most of them claimed they must have filled out the manifest wrong.'

'That can happen. I myself am poor at basic admin tasks. Jenkins over in Narcotics is *hopeless*. He has a child called "Herpes" as a direct result of his inability to fill out a form correctly.'

'I thought, perhaps with some further investigation ...'

'Officer Clag, don't take this the wrong way,' Peterson steepled his fingers and smiled in an annoying beatific way, 'But do you think, that just possibly, you're clutching at straws? Trying to find some intrigue where there isn't really any intrigue to be found? I know that you find life a little *quiet* around these parts.'

Phoebe felt her last vestige of enthusiasm slip away, and she slumped against the wall. A ventilation pipe dripped onto her epaulette. 'I suppose I might be reading too much into the situation.'

Peterson leaned back and exhaled a long, deep breath, which was a sure sign that a speech of some kind was looming.

'Do you know why there's so little customs and excise crime in this system?'

Phoebe was about to start listing all the obvious reasons: the lack of passing space traffic, the system not really being on the way to anywhere, the populace's general lack of imagination, the dearth of any commodities worth smuggling, and so on, but instead she bit her lip and waited for Peterson to impart his wisdom.

'It's *love*, that's the key. We let them know they're loved,' he pointed to the poster on the wall which showed a Police Viper shooting a beam of hearts and rainbows at a smiling pirate, who was cradling a Labrador. One of the recent police initiatives had been to give suspected criminals a pet to look after. It was supposed, Phoebe vaguely remembered, to teach them responsibility or something. Most of the dogs were now just wandering around the space station corridors, having gone feral, weeing on the carpets and biting people. 'It's not a them-and-us situation,' Peterson continued. 'You've got to see the good in citizens, even the smugglers and the villains and your basic ne'er-do-wells. Crush them with human kindness.'

Phoebe shrugged. She didn't buy it, but she'd heard worse philosophies.

'Your misplaced zeal and desire for Things To Happen doesn't really chime with our softly, softly approach.'

'It's just so *boring*,' said Phoebe. 'That's the trouble.'

'Have you considered taking up a hobby?' said Peterson with a sympathetic cock of his head. 'Hobbies are great. Take me, for example – I'm writing a thriller. It's a novel, but I think it has real movie potential, because I have a naturally visual brain. Comes from my years of looking at things with a policeman's eye. Much harder than you'd think, the writing. You have to make everything up. Like, the ship that the hero pilots. What colour is that ship?'

The sergeant paused. Phoebe wasn't sure if this was an actual question.

'Green?' she suggested, helpfully.

'Could be green. Could be blue. It's those telling details that bring the prose to life.'

'Thank you, sir. I'll try to keep all that in mind,' said Phoebe.

'The problem with you, Officer Clag, is you don't have enough of a life outside your job. I never see you out and about around the station. What is it you *do* with your free time? To relax, I mean?'

I sit on my rented massage couch in my tiny apartment and I eat synthi-noodles and sometimes have borderline psychotic thoughts about the stains in my shirt.

'I read a lot,' said Phoebe.

'Well, you need to let your hair down. There's an Outsider Art public view on at the Omar Sharif Jazz Lounge tonight. Go along! Meet people! That's an order. I'm *ordering* you as your superior. I don't think I can technically do that, but I'm doing it anyway.'

* * *

There was no sign of Officer Clag's Police Viper as Misha pulled into the *Jim Bergerac*, which at least meant she didn't see him prang the side of the docking bay again. As he resignedly watched the soundless shower of sparks and waited for the automatic fine to pop up on his screen, he could already hear Misha Senior's looming admonishment. *'Why are you so poor at the docking? By which I mean both the real docking, and also the* metaphorical *docking. The metaphorical docking is with* women. *If threshing machine accident had not left your mother with no tear ducts I know she would sob in grave.'*

Misha loitered around the bay for a while, hoping Phoebe would turn up, pretending to do some last minute checks on the livestock. He fiddled with the flight console. He read through his tax documentation a few times. After an hour with no sign of her, he gave up. Another bust, which meant that in the past six months his interactions with Phoebe Clag had amounted to:

- Three visits to the *Jim Bergerac* without even seeing her.
- Two occasions when he had stood next to her at a vending machine but not managed to say anything.
- One occasion when he had waved at her whilst passing in a corridor. This possibly didn't count because he didn't think she had noticed the wave and he had, half-way through, tried to alter the wave into swatting an imaginary fly.
- One occasion when he had inexplicably said the word 'Yag' to her instead of 'Hi'.

He grabbed a show-pig and floated across the docking bay towards the lift.

The lift was unpleasant, both because the sensation of steadily increasing gravity as it sped from the weightless hub of the station to the outer wheel made Misha nauseous, and because the built-in biometric advertising yapped embarrassingly all the way.

'Why not try the new salad bar on level two?' suggested a shimmering poster, sensing that Misha was carrying a few pounds more than was ideal for his height.

'All you can eat chicken buckets!' suggested another, sensing the exact same thing.

'Singles night at Club Moroder,' suggested a third, using a quick blast of micro-spectroscopy that failed to find any indication of recent sexual intercourse.

The lift stopped and Vitali, another Gippsworldian, got on. He was wearing a bright white kaftan, carrying a strange pink-faced ferret thing in a basket, and there was what looked like a piece of meat taped to his conical hat. It seemed to Misha that ever since the art boom, fashions had been getting quite hard to keep a handle on.

'Misha! What's up? Still trying to shift those pigs?'

'Hi, Vitali. Yeah, still trying.' Misha pulled a what-can-you-do? face.

'Listen, forget about the pigs for a while. Me and some of the other guys have got a public view of our latest pieces going on tonight. You should come along.'

Vitali pressed a flyer into Misha's hand. 'I'm hoping some high-rollers might be there. I just sold five sculptures for thirty credits a pop. Apparently my work puts people in mind of the Neo-Bauhaus school.'

'That's wonderful,' said Misha. 'Who are the Neo-Bauhaus school?'

'I have no clue!' said Vitali, grinning. 'Crazy times!'

* * *

The market hall where traders gathered to do their trading was packed, but not with the kind of people who looked like they wanted to buy pigs. Misha found his way over to a spare stall, put out his pile of complimentary pig-shaped branded key rings, and punched in his asking price, which flashed neon on the screen above his head. Looking round, it was apparent he was the only one in the entire room not buying or selling Gippsworld art. Well-heeled types glanced at him pityingly. A beautiful platinum blonde almost tripped up over his show-pig.

'Sorry,' said Misha, pulling the pig out of the way.

'What the hell is *that*?' said the platinum blonde.

'It's a Gippsworld Virtual Pig. Are you interested in substitute pork, by any chance?'

'Some of it is on my shoe.'

41

'You can try a free sample if you like. Guaranteed best on Gippsworld.'

The platinum blonde looked at him as if the distance between them was an infinite number of light-years rather than a few inches, which Misha supposed it might as well be.

'Bulgakov Trading, outstanding in our field,' he called half-heartedly after her as she turned away. 'Field, like fields on a farm.'

The rest of the afternoon crawled by glacially. The only offer Misha had was when a bored-looking teen approached his trading terminal and punched in the momentarily staggering amount of 55378008 credits for the herd. Then the teen cackled and said 'Boobless', before walking off whistling. Selling pigs could be pretty demeaning. Misha waited another two hours before packing up. He looked at the flyer Vitali had given him. He could, he decided, use a drink.

* * *

'Mister Misha!' said the manager of the Omar Sharif Jazz Lounge, smiling in a way that showed off a lot of new radium-capped teeth. 'So good to see you again.'

'Hi, Yevgeny,' said Misha, blanching at the huge throng in front of him.

'I am afraid we have no chicken buckets today because of the art-show.'

'No, that's fine.'

'I know how much you like your chicken buckets.'

'Thanks, Yevgeny, really – just here for a drink.'

The Omar Sharif Jazz Lounge, formerly Xanadu's, formerly The Hole In The Wall, took up an entire service module that had been welded into place over an actual hole in the wall where an asteroid had smacked into the station years before. It didn't usually attract much of a crowd. But with the art-boom and sudden influx of a Better Class of Person, the management, recognising a business opportunity when they saw one, had changed the carpets and spruced up the décor, and now it hardly stank of congealed chip-fat at all. Music banged, courtesy of Myq-L and the Bimblefunks, a band that a popular Foster System magazine had described as anthropologically interesting and rhythmically confusing. An unsettling, surgery-based video installation beamed across the walls. Vitali was there in the middle of the room, holding forth to an enthralled gaggle of journalists. 'I suppose, if this work is to be remembered for anything in a hundred years' time,' he was saying, 'then I hope it is for daring to tell *the truth*. Also the hands, which came out well, considering how tricky hands are.' Misha almost turned straight back the way he'd come, but across the club, past the bewildering hats and the pedestals topped off with lumps of Gippsworld mud, he spotted her.

Phoebe Clag stood in the corner, studying one of the exhibits intently, a frown on her face. Dynamic shampoo was making her hair cycle through a bunch of different colours in the way that had been fashionable a few years before. It seemed as if she wasn't talking to anybody. A baristabot banged into Misha's elbow, so he waved his credit ID at it, scooped up a fancy cocktail and some canapés from its little silver platter, and sidled in Phoebe's direction as quickly as he could without looking like he was walking straight over to her. Once he'd got to within a couple of feet he realised that this was as far as his plan went. He did a sort of half-smile, but his mouth was so dry his lip got stuck to his gum and it came out more like a leering grimace. He stared at the artwork in front of them. According to the little card next to it the title of the piece

43

was *Prometheus, Reclining, Contemplates The Howling Void.* It looked a bit like a crow, or possibly a bat, only with a pumpkin for a head. A minute went by with the two of them just staring at Prometheus. Misha was trying to decide whether 'It's a bold interpretation of a difficult subject, don't you think?' was a better opening gambit than, 'It's true what they say: without art, we have no identity,' when, with a crunching sound of metal on bone, Phoebe kicked him hard in the shin.

'Laika's mother!' yelped Misha, dropping his canapés.

'Oh, god, I'm so sorry!' said Phoebe, putting her hand over her mouth and turning bright red. 'Are you okay?'

'It's fine,' said Misha, blinking back tears. 'It's nothing.'

'You're bleeding!'

'Don't worry. I bleed much too easily. My fault, really.'

'You bleed too easily? Oh *god*. Should I get a medibot?'

'No, I don't mean I've got a condition, I just – forget about it.' Misha smiled and tried not to wince at the same time. 'I don't even like these trousers anyway,' he added, wiping pointlessly at the blossoming bloodstain with his sleeve.

'Well, geez – sorry again,' said Phoebe, shooting her cybernetic leg a mortified look. 'It keeps doing that lately. I need to get it serviced.'

They both went back to awkwardly studying the sculpture. In the background the anthropologically interesting band finished a song about a Gippsworld potato blight and started a new song about plague sanitation.

Misha, after the pain in his shin had subsided enough for him to be able to speak properly, eventually nodded at Prometheus. 'This puts me in mind of the Neo-Bauhaus school,' he said.

'Oh, does it?' said Phoebe, blinking. 'I don't think I know them. What are they about?'

'Well, lots of things. Hard to put into words. Being attuned to nature, that's one of the main issues. Like here – with the way it has those … bits stuck to it.'

'Right, definitely,' said Phoebe. 'It's very clever. The bits. Makes you think.'

'It does. It makes you think.'

The conversation lapsed.

'You don't see many cybernetic limbs these days,' said Misha, after another excruciating minute had ticked by.

Phoebe nodded, and stared at the floor. 'Most people assume it signifies gigantic mental issues.'

'Not at all! It's just – that's to say – it's none of my business, but I wondered – not that it's important – but, you know, I *noticed* and I wondered …'

'Why don't I let them grow me a new one?'

'Yes.'

'Gigantic mental issues.'

'Oh.'

Misha looked hard at the back of his own hand. Phoebe drained her drink. 'So, are you one of the artists?' she asked.

'No. I'm in the trading business,' said Misha. 'Importing and exporting.'

'What sort of stuff?'

'Oh, you know, different things. Mainly quite niche products. Luxury items, I suppose you could call them.'

OR PIGS. PIGS. YOU COULD CALL THEM PIGS, his inner monologue shouted. Misha hated his inner monologue and was used to ignoring it. Detecting empty glasses, another baristabot bobbled up to them.

'Hey, let me get these,' said Misha, waving his ID at its head. He went to grab two more drinks, but the readout on the machine's tuxedo flashed red.

45

'Insufficient funds,' said the baristabot, who wasn't programmed for tact. Misha waved the card again.

'There should be at least five credits left on there,' he protested.

'Insufficient funds.'

'How much are these drinks?'

'Ten credits.'

'*What?*'

Phoebe leaned forward, waved her ID, and the readout flashed green. She took the cocktails and handed him one.

'It's kind of crazy, isn't it?' she said. 'Prices have gone *bonkers* here since this whole Outsider Art fad. It's like, two hundred percent inflation or something.'

'I forgot that I'd put most of my cash on the other card,' said Misha, by way of explanation. 'The cash that I make from the importing and the exporting.'

'No, sure, of course,' Phoebe said with a nod. 'I've made that mistake myself.'

The conversation hit a third, seemingly inescapable lull. Misha sighed. He made a show of checking the time, and tried to do a facial expression that signified he had an important appointment to get to as part of a full, vibrant life.

'I lost it when I was nine,' Phoebe suddenly blurted, just as he was turning to go, 'trying to impress a lanky boy called Phil by inventing a new playground game. Jump Over the Plasma Beam Generator. It wasn't a great game, didn't catch on. But when I woke up with a new leg grafted into place I freaked out. I became *convinced* it was haunted, like it was some sort of *ghost* leg, and that it was going to try to kick me to death in my sleep.'

'That's understandable,' said Misha, thinking that it sounded pretty weird.

'My mum found me in the bathroom trying to cut it off with a spatula. Hadn't got very far. In my unbalanced state I'd chosen utensils poorly.'

'I can imagine that's easily done.'

'They packed me off to a lot of expensive psychologists, but that didn't work out. I decided it was all part of a shadowy conspiracy. Eventually, after a few more increasingly messy attempts at leg removal, my mother got tired of having to repaint the bathroom, and managed to find a surgeon who'd agree to re-amputate and fit me with this.' She pointed at the metal leg. 'The hydraulics keep breaking down, sourcing spare parts is a nightmare. On the upside, I can keep sandwiches in my thigh compartment.'

'That's good. I like sandwiches,' said Misha, instantly realising this wasn't the sort of personal detail that impressed women.

'He is also big fan of chicken buckets,' said Yevgeny, wandering past and winking at Phoebe. 'We call him Mister Chicken Buckets. One of our best customers. Enjoy your evening.'

Misha gulped at his drink and thought about lingering death.

'So, Mister Chicken Buckets,' said Phoebe. 'Tell me more about the glamorous space trading business.'

* * *

Misha felt weirdly disembodied as he listened to himself talk. Partly it was the cocktails; mostly it was his brain's attempt to try to insulate itself from the full horror of what was unfolding. He'd stood powerlessly by as he heard his mouth spend ten minutes explaining how prone he was to nosebleeds when adjusting to the space station's centrifugal gravity. Then he heard it move from that topic onto a graphic description of his childhood bowel problems. Now, in some inexplicably inept attempt to change the conversational course it appeared to have resorted to regaling Phoebe with anecdotes lifted directly from Cliff Ganymede's autobiography *The Moon's A Balloon (Watch Out, Fake Moon! It's A Thargoid Trap!)*.

'... so that's when the Pilots' Federation made me the youngest pilot in the entire star system to be awarded the rank of Deadly. Which was a real honour. And did I mention that I fly a top-of-the-range Anaconda? Because that is also a thing I do.'

He wondered if she'd noticed the horseshoes of sweat on his shirt. He was wearing the latest gland-freeze spray, but there was only so much you could ask of it. *There is a chance she hasn't noticed*, Misha thought, *so long as her eyeballs are just painted marbles, like on a taxidermied crow, and she's faking being able to see.*

He tried not to think about the fact that once out of his sight it would take her five seconds to call up every detail about his employment history, income, mental health, and – given another half a minute or so – probably an entire run-down of all his recessive genes. Though it might take her a little while to work her way through the list, because he had many.

'But, goodness, I seem to have talked quite a lot. What about you? Do you enjoy police work?'

'Good grief. Is it that obvious?'

'What?'

'That I'm a cop?' Phoebe wrinkled her nose. 'Can you tell by my feet or something?'

'No, I, uh, think I must have seen you doing a docking bay inspection. I notice that sort of thing because of the importing and exporting. For which, noticing skills are important. It must be exciting. Catching criminals, busting smuggling operations?'

'It's quieter than you might expect.' Phoebe shrugged. 'There's been a bit of low-level smuggling since Placet B passed that Madeleine law.'

'Madeleine law?'

'Like the cakes.'

'They banned cakes?' Misha said, lost.

'Not literally. It's a nickname. Because of Proust.'

Misha tried to nod his head in the way he imagined a man who had read Proust might do.

'Apparently, hundreds of years ago,' Phoebe started to explain, 'when they didn't have so much in the way of instant reproduction tech, you'd have to just … remember stuff. People didn't have recordings of everything they ever did. Product packaging would change, and everyone would get wistful for it. If you go back far enough there were actual entire shows and movies that had been lost. Obviously that's before we sent out ships to pick up all the old radio waves. Anyhow, people would forget that stuff was rubbish; they'd sort of imagine everything with this kind of rosy glow they called "nostalgia". And they felt happy thinking about how good things were, and they felt happy bitching about how terrible things were today by comparison. So to get the sense of nostalgia back, on Placet B they've tried to ban any technology or recorded material designated a non-vital cultural artefact that's more than thirty years old.'

'Wow, that seems extreme. Does it work?'

'Not really. It's a pretty ridiculous and unworkable law. But at least it means that every so often I get to find a hidden database of old movies and slap them with a fine. It's not, to be honest, what I saw myself doing at this stage in life.'

49

She knocked back another drink, and continued glumly, 'Do you ever think that there's like a hyper-loop shuttle, and that all your peers got on the shuttle at the point they were meant to, but somehow you didn't, you missed it, and now you're stuck on the platform and there are no other shuttles coming ever again? Do you think you can mess up your life because of one stupid mistake? Sorry, that's a daft question. You're a successful importer-exporter of niche luxury items.'

'Well, yes, but that's not to say I've not had my share of disappointments,' said Misha, wishing he had dialled it back a little. 'What was it?'

'What was what?'

'Your mistake?'

Phoebe bit her lip. 'It was my dissertation. For my final year Policing Exams. Up to that point, I'd pretty much aced everything. Top marks at theory, attendance, badge polishing. A star student across the board. And then I decided to write a thesis about the history of Galcop. You know the old Coriolis stations? I went through a bunch of operations logs, and it turns out the police back in those days were total imbeciles. I mean, unfathomably stupid. If there was an alert, the standard practice – which had been drawn up by this Commissioner Osborne guy, the real bigwig – anyway, the standard practice was just to fly out of the station regardless of any intel. Half the time the perp would simply *park* there, waiting, and pick the cops' Vipers off one by one. Crazy casualty levels! The sort of thing mad generals in the bad old days would have approved of. So I wrote a scathing account of what a giant idiot Commissioner Osborne must have been.'

She downed another drink.

'Clever Clag. Didn't bother to think about the fact the current police chief's surname is also Osborne. The famous

50

historical idiot turned out to be her grandfather. So, long story short, I've been stuck here for the last two years.'

'Ah,' Misha tried to think of something better and more comforting to say than 'ah', failed and so just said 'Ah' again.

'Hold this. I'll be back in a second,' said Phoebe.

* * *

She slumped down in the toilet cubicle, turned the dial of the drug dispenser to 'Neurotic', and necked a couple of mood pills. Then she slapped herself hard in the side of the head. What, she wondered, was *wrong* with her? She had finally talked to the guy from the vending machine with the pleasant, open face, who turned out to be both successful and *multilingual*, because he'd definitely said 'yag' instead of 'hello' that last time they'd spoken, and now she was messing it up by being miserable and by making weird shuttle metaphors and by sharing too much about her dysmorphia issues. And, to cap it all, there was obviously a bug in her neural link, because that was the third time the leg had gone on the fritz and she'd booted somebody. The trigger seemed to be whenever she found herself in an awkward social situation. Which, she realised gloomily, meant it was going to happen a lot.

She blinked on her police crime scene recorder, guiltily sped past the NOT FOR PERSONAL USE warning boxes, and a ream of data about the evening scrolled past her face. This kind of thing was ethically dubious, but she was so poor at judging facial cues she could justify it to herself as simply levelling the playing field. She was pleased to see that Misha's eye dilation and sweat levels suggested either a fatal pituitary disease of some sort or a 70% chance that he was interested in her. *Jesus Christ*, she thought, as more biometric data scrolled past, *he has a LOT of recessive genes*. Glen's almost flawless DNA flashed into her mind for a moment before she had a chance to stamp the image down. A nice-looking double helix wasn't everything. She undid the top button of her shirt and wished she'd changed it earlier. Hopefully the noodle-stain looked like a deliberate bit of design. Perhaps she could pass it off as *avant-garde*. It's not like some of these Gippsworld artists weren't wearing enough crazy crap.

Heading back across the throbbing Jazz Lounge, Phoebe was so busy worrying about the stain that she didn't notice a rowdy new group at the bar until a terrible, piercing shriek stopped her in her tracks.

'Fffeeeeeeeeeebbbbbbssss!'

Phoebe froze.

'Alicia!' she said, turning around and doing the best approximation of a grin she could manage in the circumstances.

Alicia, just as bony and glossy as she remembered, did weird little air kisses either side of Phoebe's head and pulled her towards where a gaggle of homicide detectives were shouting and downing shots and giving each other high-fives. Phoebe could tell they were homicide because they were all wearing their stupid shiny homicide division bomber jackets. A slightly confused but glassily cheery Peterson was there too. He raised a wobbly drink at her.

'Soooo great to see you! You didn't reply to my message!' Alicia shrieked again, right into Phoebe's ear this time. 'Have a drink, we're celebrating!'

'Oh, Alicia, I'd love to,' said Phoebe, 'but I've got a *thing*.'

'Nonsense! You never have a thing,' Alicia turned to Peterson and tugged his sleeve. 'Tell her she has to stay!'

'Your future career progression depends on it,' said Peterson, with a ponderous nod. Facial cues went on letting Phoebe down, so she couldn't tell if he was joking and reluctantly let herself get dragged into the middle of the group. Alicia sloshed out some thick green juice from a bottle into a cocktail glass.

'Have some Lavian gin! It's really expensive! Because it's fermented in the guts of marmosets or civets or something!'

'I think I read that it kills the civets,' said Phoebe, frowning. 'It's actually a very cruel process.'

'I know! I read that too! Isn't that brilliant? It's why it's so exclusive.'

Phoebe looked through the throng to where Misha was still loitering, studying a complimentary vol-au-vent. She waved. He waved back. Phoebe pulled an apologetic face, rolled her eyes theatrically, mouthed the words 'work stuff' and held up a hand to indicate five minutes. Misha gave her a thumbs-up and mouthed 'no problem'. Then he did a little mime. At least, Phoebe thought it was a mime, it could have been an epileptic fit or something. She had no clue what it was supposed to convey, but she grinned at him anyway.

'It's great down this end of the station,' said Alicia. 'So much more urban. The way you've got *litter* in the corridors. Our neighbourhood is so clean and anodyne. Such a good choice of venue for an art show, it's got real edge.'

'Yes, we don't see you guys round here very often.'

'Today's a special occasion!'

The homicide detectives chest-bumped and gave themselves another round of high-fives.

'What are you celebrating?' Phoebe asked.

'We've closed the Cliff Ganymede case! Our division's hundred percent clean-up record goes on standing!'

53

Alicia whooped and the homicide jocks made a sort of boo-yah noise.

'Hey, that's fantastic, congratulations,' Phoebe said, not even trying to sound like she meant it. 'So … who did it?'

'Did what?'

'The murder.'

'Nobody!' shrieked Alicia. 'It turns out it was a suicide all along!'

'A suicide?' Phoebe stared at her, blankly. 'But he was *beaten* to death with a copy of his own book.'

'Yes, that's right. We're working on the theory that he beat himself to death.'

'What about the *anonymous hit* that had been placed on him? The bounty offered on one of the pirate message boards?'

'Yes, well, we couldn't get any leads on that,' said Alicia, with an airy shrug, 'So we figured it was probably a hit placed by Ganymede himself, to make it *look* like a murder.'

Phoebe goggled at her. 'But … why? Why would he do that?'

'Because he was mentally unbalanced, obviously. You've got to remember that the guy must have been *suicidal* to kill himself, so that makes you do strange, unexplainable things. And he was a writer. Writers are messed up.'

'Don't take this the wrong way, Alicia. It just … it doesn't really sound plausible.'

Alicia sniffed. 'Gee, Phoebe, it's great to have your input. And I'm sure there are lots of things that you know – about *customs* and *excise*. If I had a customs and excise question I'd definitely come to you. But this is, or rather *isn't*, a homicide, and we're homicide detectives, so I *kind of* think we know what we're doing. Besides, I heard you have your own super-exciting, poorly-filled-out-cargo-manifest case to deal with. But anyway, let's not talk about that. Ganymede's not the only big news. Can you keep a secret?'

Phoebe nodded, and felt her stomach knot.

'I shouldn't be telling you – it's embargoed until next week – but I'm on the shortlist. For the "thirty police under thirty to watch out for" thing.'

'Oh. Fuck. I mean, wow. That's really excellent, Alicia.'

Alicia flicked her flicky hair back. 'I love this outfit by the way! You look like you're going to a children's party. It's so Phoebe! It's really refreshing how you don't care about your appearance.'

* * *

Misha had made the final centimetre of his drink last for the best part of twenty minutes, but he didn't think he could pretend to be engrossed in *Prometheus, Reclining, Contemplates The Howling Void* for much longer. He chanced another quick look towards the bar, where Phoebe was still chatting with her friends. Probably, Misha thought, his shoulders drooping, she had called them from the toilet. *Please rescue me, I'm trapped talking to a man who won't quit flapping his gums about the spaceship he obviously doesn't really own.* And what was with that ludicrous attempt to mime being 'shot through the heart' just then? Where had *that* come from? He ran his hand through his hair, and a bit of vegetable gristle dropped out. *You have pig guts on you. She's not coming back. You've blown it in the space of an hour. When you get back home you're going to top yourself by jumping into the Gippsworld mineshaft.*

The club was starting to thin out. Misha waved for a baristabot to bring him another cocktail, then remembered that he couldn't afford it. He ordered a slightly cheaper perception filter instead, so that at least his recollection of

55

the evening would have the more appalling edges softened. He sat at an empty table, peeled off the back of the filter, stuck it to his arm, and was about to resign himself to another night alone with *Mission: Thargoid Kill-Punch* when he felt a tap on his shoulder.

'Excuse me.'

Misha looked up. It took him a little while to place her. It was the dazzlingly beautiful platinum blonde from the market hall.

'Hello,' said the dazzlingly beautiful platinum blonde, flashing a dazzling smile to match the rest of her face. 'I couldn't help but hear you talking about your thriving intergalactic space-trading business earlier.'

'Yes,' said Misha, shaking his head, as a wave of self-disgust crashed up against the perception filter and easily overpowered it, because the Omar Sharif Jazz Lounge watered their product down pretty badly. 'I was talking about that.'

'Can I buy you a drink?' The blonde sat down next to him and put her mouth very close to his ear. 'I've got a proposition for you.'

Chapter Five

Phoebe rubbed her eyes, popped another sobriety pill and decided that, in retrospect, those civets and their endangered digestive tracts deserved everything they got. She wasn't a hundred percent sure how the rest of the evening had progressed. She remembered getting trapped in an argument with Alicia about the merits of an entirely noodle-based diet. She remembered noticing Misha talking to an irritatingly beautiful platinum blonde, and she remembered that by the time she'd finally got free from the homicide goons he had vanished. She remembered Sergeant Peterson explaining his theories on story structure, which somehow tied in to why he thought pugs were a lazy type of dog. She had a dim recollection that she might have agreed to read his unfinished novel. That was the bit that was making her anxious, so even though it wasn't on the schedule, she decided to take a ship out and patrol the dead space around the station; that way she could avoid her boss and hopefully nobody would try to talk to her.

She chose Police Viper number six like always, because it had an ammonia leak coming out of the starboard wingtip that maintenance never seemed to fix. Phoebe had become pretty adept at timing it so that with a few spins and twists she could leave behind a fleeting floating gas doodle in the vacuum. Sometimes she drew famous landmarks. Sometimes she drew actor's faces. Most of the time she drew genitals. She wasn't particularly proud of herself, but it was still a skill.

After a couple of hours she got bored of the space doodling, and decided she should probably at least go through the motions of her actual job. She scanned a readout showing all the traffic coming and going from the *Jim Bergerac* that day. A methane shipment. Some Indigenous Outsider Art. Some more Indigenous Outsider Art. Methane. Art. Art. Methane. Art. Then a name caught her eye:

```
Misha Bulgakov — Transport Barn — Pig (substi-
tute)
```

And before she really had time to think about it, she found herself beaming across a message.

```
Ahoy. This is Officer Phoebe Clag of the Jim
Bergerac's C&E division! Prepare to be boarded!
```

Misha didn't reply, but a *Ready* code meekly signalled his acquiescence, and his ship slowed to a crawl as her computer, in turn, automatically matched his pace and fired out a wobbly docking tunnel.

Phoebe scrolled through the rest of his ID. She frowned.

```
Pilot's Rating: Harmless
Violations: 19 tickets for Minor Docking
Damage, 1 health and safety citation for cabin
fungal residue.
Payload: Pigs (substitute)
Previous 50 payloads: Pigs (substitute)
```

For a moment she thought that maybe it was a different Misha. But then his picture flashed up, and there he was, looking slightly lumpier and pastier than she recalled from the night before, but definitely him. According to the log, his ship – designated Transport-Barn *Malkovich,* the sole ship for which he had a licence – hadn't ever gone more than thirty miles from Gippsworld. And his trading history suggested that his import-export business empire was limited mostly to export, and the luxury items were limited entirely to the pigs. Phoebe excitedly straightened her police hat and brushed some of the previous night's noodles off her jacket. Nobody had bothered lying to her for ages.

* * *

'Hi there! Unexpected spot-check!' she said, stepping through the airlock and flashing him both her badge and a nervous grin. Misha's stricken, sweaty face instantly made her regret the whole idea. It had seemed as if it would be cute a few moments earlier, but the poor guy, obviously mortified about being shown up, looked like he was ready to puke.

'Hi there,' he said weakly, waving her through into the ship's cramped, little cabin.

'I guess the top-of-the-line Anaconda is at home for the day!' She meant that to sound like a breezy shared joke, but as soon as it was out of her mouth she worried it had come out like a dig, because Misha just stared miserably at his shoes. Phoebe coughed awkwardly. 'Sorry about running off last night. My colleagues are a bit hard to escape.'

'Sure, no problem,' mumbled Misha.

'I can't even remember the details of half the stuff you and me were talking about, by the way,' she lied. 'That Lavian brandy goes straight to my head. Seems like I don't have hollow legs!' She tapped her metal leg in a self-depre-cating way, but he didn't say anything. Perhaps, thought Phoebe, sinkingly, it would be best to just act business-like and get this over with as quickly as possible.

'So, let's check out the cargo, shall we?'

Misha, still avoiding any eye contact whatsoever, led her through to the hold. About forty Gippsworld pigs, not blessed with magno-boots – unlike their human companions – were bobbing around, gently bumping into each other, letting out odd snorts.

'I'm sorry about the smell,' said Misha. 'Away from Gippsworld they start to go off a bit. Though, to be honest, they don't smell that great to start off with.'

'You know, in all the time I've been posted here, I never thought to ask – who actually *buys* these things?' said Phoebe, gingerly tapping one that was drifting towards her head.

'Mainly they're sold as a bacon substitute to the more fundamentalist planets that would quite like to eat some bacon but whose religions forbid them to eat either actual pigs or printed synthetic products,' he replied robotically.

'Sounds lucrative,' she said, flicking through the manifest.

'Not really. They're a poor product. I mean they *act* vaguely like pigs, and the flesh seems a little like pork, so long as you just look at it and don't put it in your mouth, but that's about as far as it goes.'

'What do they taste like?'

'Bark. Sponge. Burnt rubber. You have to do a lot of chewing. Usually, once a planet has tasted its first Gippsworld Virtual Pig the inhabitants either decide they can do without pork substitute after all, or they change their founding religious texts right there and then to allow the real stuff and to ban our version. We don't get much in the way of repeat business.'

Yikes, thought Phoebe. *He's REALLY sweating. Even worse than in the club.* She didn't think she'd ever seen a human being sweat so much. And his hands were shaking. She averted her eyes, embarrassed for him.

'Anything else I should know about?' Phoebe asked, as she wandered around the hold, making a show of banging on things in a professional-looking way. She tugged her lapels in a pantomime of an old-fashioned detective. 'I notice that you seem slightly ill at ease.'

Again, she thought that maybe by making a joke of it, she'd get him to relax a little. It didn't work out like that. Misha wobbled in his magno-boots and covered his face with his hands.

'I'm sorry! I'm *so* sorry!' He rocked back and forth. He let out a strangulated gasp. Appalled, Phoebe realised that he was crying. She had a sudden flashback to the school field trip when Bobby Osher had refused to come out of the Imperial Fortress on Proxima 6 until she agreed to hold his hand at break. The teacher had made her go along with it and she could still remember Bobby's terrible, clammy palms, and the way he'd clumsily tried to lick her cheek afterwards. Worst of all she remembered the distraught look on his face after she had pushed him into the hyper-moat.

'Hey, look, don't worry. People exaggerate things when they've had a drink; it's not the worst crime in the galaxy.'

But Misha wasn't listening; he was just babbling on.

'I've never done anything like this before! I don't know what came over me! I just agreed to drop it off. She said it was antiquities, you know – like a fancy vase or something – nothing bad, no *drugs* or anything like that. It won't be a big deal, that's what she said. Oh *god.*'

Phoebe's mind rewound a bit.

'Drop what off, Misha?' she asked, levelly.

Misha crossed over to the astronavigation console, opened a small refrigeration unit, and pulled a squat, black box out from where it was hidden behind a pile of pork samples.

'Oh god. Oh god. I'm going to *jail.*'

61

He handed her the box. It vibrated gently in her hands as she flipped it over a few times. She gave it a quick scan with her sonic truncheon but already knew that was pointless. This was a fancy bit of hardware; she could tell that because of the label on the side. It boasted, in a series of perky bullet points, about the impregnable polycarbide shell, the lead lining designed to block any sort of readings, and, most impressively, about the unbreakable Quantum Lenslok. It didn't take Phoebe's six years of police academy to work out that it had to contain some very high-end contraband. *That explains the sweating. It's not your irresistible pheromones sending him into a tizz. What an ego on you.*

'Okay, Misha, I think you better start at the beginning.'

Misha yanked anxiously at one of his eyebrows. 'It was a woman in the bar, after you'd gone. I think I was drunk by that point. She sat down next to me and asked if I wanted to earn a bit of extra money "the easy way".'

'Can you describe her?'

Misha shrugged. 'She was sort of … a stunningly beautiful platinum blonde.'

'She wasn't *that* beautiful,' muttered Phoebe.

'What?'

'Nothing, go on.'

'She said it would be really simple. I just had to leave the station, then she'd send me some coordinates, somebody would meet me, I'd hand the thing over, it wouldn't take more than a few hours. I can't believe I've been such an idiot. How much trouble am I in?'

'It kind of depends what's in here,' said Phoebe, tapping the box.

'I've ruined my life. I had so much potential,' Misha sniffed and wiped his nose on his sleeve. 'I was going to learn a coding language.'

Phoebe tried to think of something reassuring to say about first time offences when a light on the astronavigation console started to flicker.

'Should it be doing that?' she asked.

Before Misha could reply, some other lights in the space-ship joined in, along with a bunch of alarms, all flashing and wailing like they'd scored Thargoid Madness on a Cliff Ganymede pinball machine. Alerts blared out from the flight computer: *Approaching object. Weapons targeting detected.* Other unwelcome sounding sentences.

They both swivelled their heads to stare out of the cockpit window, where an ominous silvery speck was getting bigger and bigger.

'Bother,' said Phoebe, as the speck suddenly fired a spray of yellow plasma bolts, which – eating up the space between them like a hundred eager pac-men – tore into the hull of her empty Viper. They watched it explode soundlessly. The pig transport wobbled in an invisible swell. *That's going to be a week's worth of paperwork, right there,* thought Phoebe, as dirty great chunks of her spaceship floated past the window.

'What's happening? Why is somebody shooting at us?' said Misha, sounding aggrieved.

'I don't know what you've got mixed up in, but I think it's safe to say that whatever is in this box isn't a *fancy vase*,' said Phoebe, as the hulk of their assailant's ship whooshed over the top of them.

'Should we do some sort of evasive manoeuvre?' said Misha. 'When this happens in an episode of *Galloping Ganymede!* they usually do an evasive manoeuvre.'

'We're in a barn full of pigs,' said Phoebe.

Phoebe and Misha simultaneously experienced Mixed Emotions. Phoebe's emotions were mixed because on the one hand she didn't want to die whilst she had an unused noodle coupon back in her apartment, but on the other hand this was the first exciting thing to happen in her job for as long as she could remember. Misha's emotions were mixed because on the one hand he didn't want to die without ever having kissed an actual woman on the mouth, but on the other hand he thought it was a Core Dynamics Federal Corvette that was attacking them, which was notoriously one of the really difficult starships to tick off in the *Gollancz Bumper Book of Space Going Vessels*.

'Look, we've got about thirty seconds before it swings by again,' said Phoebe. 'Where are the escape pods?'

'Over here,' Misha pointed to a bulkhead across the cabin. They ran as fast as the magno-boots would let them. Phoebe, getting there first, punched a button on the first pod. An 'Out of Order' sign blinked on. Misha looked a bit guilty.

'I haven't done a health and safety check in a little while.'

Phoebe tried escape pod number two. Another 'Out of Order' sign blinked on.

'I really did *intend* to,' said Misha. 'But you know how it is. Things crop up. Have you ever played *Mission: Thargoid Kill-Punch*?'

'Have you got any survival suits?'

'There's this,' Misha said, pulling a bulky, old-fashioned spacesuit with a large domed helmet out from a locker. 'It's for EVAs. Cleaning the solar panels and things. Look, there's a built-in jetpack. They were giving them away free at an agriculture conference.'

'But you've just got the one?'

'It's quite big. You're quite small. I think we might both be able to squeeze in at once.'

They both looked at Misha's slightly-too-chunky belly for a second.

'Well, come on then,' said Phoebe. 'We'll just have to do our best.'

They did their best to squeeze. In the process Misha accidentally pressed the override button on Phoebe's loose RemLok mask, and a big skein of protective plastic wrapped around them, like a gigantic condom.

'Sorry,' said Misha.

With a bit of wriggling they managed to get the suit zipped up. Outside, the corvette had lined up for another run, and more bright yellow dots started to zoom towards them. They waddled, like kids in a three-legged race, towards the emergency airlock bolts.

'Pull it!' said Phoebe.

Misha strained, managed to wangle a finger free from the plastic, get his arm into one of the suit's sleeves, and yank the eject lever. The bolts fired, the airlock door jettisoned off into the void, and they tumbled out after it, just as the rest of the cargo transport disintegrated under the impact of a hundred more plasma blasts. They spiralled off into nowhere, and held their breaths in the gloom, waiting to see if their attacker would notice them amongst the debris and the pigs.

'I think they've gone,' whispered Phoebe after a while. 'It should be safe to switch on the emergency distress systems.'

Misha grunted and managed to press a button with his chin. An electronic poster automatically shimmered across the visor around their heads.

'Oofff,' said Phoebe. 'Why do they fit these things with advertising?'

'Apparently, it's supposed to be relaxing,' said Misha. 'Also, I read that in a high stress situation, such as one where you're having to activate an emergency distress system, the human brain is more susceptible to buying stuff.'

'Free bucket-of-beaks chicken feast on level two of the Jim Bergerac,' chirped an advert. Misha blushed.

'Singles night at Club Moroder,' said another pop-up. This time, they both blushed.

* * *

'Why are the backpack jets not automatically firing to send us towards the nearest population centre?' said Phoebe with a frown, after another few minutes had passed. 'And why isn't the emergency beacon doing anything?'

'There is a chance,' said Misha, 'that I didn't get round to upgrading the software.'

'We're in the middle of nowhere, Misha. It could be *days* before anyone finds us. Can we at least fire a manual guidance booster?'

Misha looked at the fuel gauge, and pulled a face. 'Sorry,' he said. 'I was honestly intending to sort that one out this week.'

* * *

'Damn,' said Phoebe.

'What is it?'

She stared glumly at something in the distance. Misha couldn't really turn his face, but he tried to follow her gaze. About twenty metres away, the Lenslok box was spinning in the blackness. It seemed to be keeping pace with them but staying tantalisingly out of reach.

'That was the evidence,' said Phoebe. 'And now we're going to lose it.'

Misha thought for a moment. A sleepy-looking pig drifted in their direction. 'Hang on a second, I've got an idea,' he said. 'Look – see that pig coming towards us? Try to grab it as it goes past.'

Phoebe, with some sliding and cursing, managed to get her arm free from where it was trapped next to Misha's belly, and poked it into the other sleeve, which concertinaed out into space.

'Now I can't really see because your head is in the way,' she pointed out.

'Don't worry, I can. Hang on a moment. It's coming … hold your hand open … now!'

Phoebe felt something brush against a glove. She just caught hold of the pig's leg before it drifted past.

'So I'm holding a pig. Now what?'

'Okay, now we need to get the pig up to this side of the visor, the side opposite to where the box is.'

There was some more slightly awkward twisting. Phoebe managed to stretch and curse and press the pig up against the domed helmet. 'Now we just need a strong, focused light source,' said Misha. 'How about your eyebrow implant – does that have a torch function?'

Phoebe activated her brow projector's torch beam and maxed it out to its highest setting. She pressed her face right up against the inside of the visor, so that she was looking straight at the pig's backside squashed against the plastiglass.

'Why have I got my face pressed against the backside of this pig?' asked Phoebe, because it seemed like a reasonable question.

'Wait a moment.'

A minute ticked by. Phoebe recoiled with a gasp as the pig exploded in a messy, gaseous shower, and they slowly rolled away in the exact opposite direction, towards the box.

'Hooray for Newtonian physics,' said Misha, feeling momentarily triumphant, as he scooped up the Lenslok on their way past.

'It's quite pretty really, isn't it?' he added, watching the trail of pig innards silently drift past them.

'In a way,' said Phoebe, dubiously.

* * *

They floated for a while. The tiny shimmering dot that was the space station possibly got a little closer, or possibly got further away; Misha couldn't really tell. Phoebe's breath was hot on his face in an alarming sort of way. His nose was pressed up into her ear. A bit of her hair had gotten into his mouth. He tried to blow it out.

'I'm not blowing on your neck – I've got some of your hair in my mouth,' he explained.

Phoebe didn't say anything. It seemed to Misha as if she was maybe in a bit of a mood. A warning alert began to flash, accompanied by a gentle dinging noise.

'Warning,' said the warning alert. 'Cartridge requires replacing! Oxygen will run out in ten minutes.'

Phoebe groaned. 'Of *course* it will.'

Misha stared guiltily out at the distant stars.

'I'm sorry my hand is sort of touching your boob, by the way,' he said.

'Don't worry about it.'

There was another difficult silence. Misha desperately tried to come up with some interesting conversation.

'So,' he said eventually, 'I've been thinking of writing a novel.'

'Fucking hell,' said Phoebe.

Chapter Six

'Misha, you are a great galactic hero to the human race,' said the Thargoid Queen, waggling her mandibles. 'In you, and you alone, we truly met our match. But now that my hive-mind legion of Thargoid drones has finally bested you in battle, we cannot let you return to your people, so we are keeping you here in this luxurious zoo enclosure, which has all the mod-cons.'

'Damn you to hell, you insect monsters,' Misha shouted, rattling the bars of his cage. 'Damn you to *hell*.'

The Thargoid Queen laughed a terrible Thargoid laugh, which was the same as a human laugh but with more mucus. Omninutrients gurgled through an organo-processor pipe. Her carapace glistened. She blinked her dozen eyes, which were black and dead, like the eyes of a games journalist or a shark.

'Whilst here in the zoo, you and the female police human will mate vigorously, so that we may better understand your strange, disgusting mammalian biology,' said the Queen.

Phoebe stepped into the cage wearing a wispy off-the-shoulder thing, and put a hand on Misha's cheek.

'Hey, let's face it, it's no use trying to resist the Thargoids,' she said, with a wink. 'We might as well go along with this.'

'There are also as many chicken buckets as you can eat,' added the Thargoid Queen. She waved a proboscis at a big pile of chicken buckets.

'Fine,' seethed Misha. 'Just this once I'll succumb to your obscene alien wishes, but don't start thinking it sets a precedent.'

* * *

Something sharp jabbed him in the neck. Misha opened his eyes. It wasn't an insectoid Thargoid appendage attempting to wrap him in some grim symbiotic mind-fuse cocoon, it was a tiny medibot with an adrenaline syringe, which promptly buzzed away when he flapped his arm at it. He looked around and saw Phoebe floating next to him. Inexplicably, it seemed, they weren't in the spacesuit anymore.

'What happened?' said Misha, groggily trying to work out where he was.

'I don't know,' said Phoebe. 'I think we must have passed out from the lack of oxygen.'

'But we're not dead.'

'No.'

'How would that work, then?'

'It looks,' said Phoebe, indicating the airlock in which they were bobbing about, 'like somebody picked us up.'

'Do you think it's Thargoids?' Misha whispered.

'What? No. Why would it be *Thargoids*?'

'Zoo exhibit. They might want us for a sexy zoo exhibit.'

'Are you okay, Misha?' She waved her hand across his face. 'You're not really making sense. I think you might have hypoxia.'

The inner door of the airlock hissed open. A sinister *tapping* sound echoed down the corridor outside. Someone or something was coming towards them. Phoebe and Misha braced themselves, as much as you could in zero gravity. The tapping grew louder.

A hen, wearing tiny magno boots, stepped into the

airlock. It looked up at them, or down at them – stupid bloody space, thought Misha – and opened its beak.

'FIT GIRL,' said the hen.

Misha and Phoebe stared at each other. They stared at the hen again.

'BITCHES GONNA BITCH,' said the hen.

Then it turned and went back the way it had come. Two pairs of human-sized magno-boots flipped out of the wall on a spindly robotic arm and waved themselves in an obvious way.

'What should we do?' said Misha, terrified.

Phoebe shrugged. 'I suppose we follow the rude hen.'

They pulled on the boots and climbed through the airlock door, as a decontamination spray did its thing. A little way ahead of them, at the far end of the corridor, the hen rounded a corner and disappeared from view again. They went on following it. Another door opened into a gloomy sort of waiting room. It smelt of oil. They both tried their best to avoid looking at the gigantic, digital wall mural, which showed a dizzying series of dancing skull-and-cross-bones, clacking their jaws and winking menacingly. The words 'ABANDON ALL HOPE' were written beneath the mural in a really unwelcoming font.

'I don't much like that font,' said Misha.

'No,' agreed Phoebe. 'I think it's the fact it's made out of actual shrunken heads.'

'Space pirates! We're done for. We're going to get eaten by space pirates.'

'Pirates don't *eat* people, Misha.'

'Well, that depends, doesn't it? I heard they eat people in the Orion system.'

'They're not cannibals in the Orion system. That's actu-ally kind of racist. I've been to Orion Beta. They have a

71

nail salon and a branch of *Zappp's*. I think people on Gippsworld should probably try to get out more.'

A scream wafted through the ventilation grill.

'But I admit,' said Phoebe, 'that I'm not an expert or anything.'

At the far end of the room another door began to slide open. Phoebe pulled out her sonic truncheon, and crouched down. Misha dropped to the floor behind her. A passage from one of Cliff Ganymede's dating books, *Getting To Third Base During A Transhuman Apocalypse* – about how relationships forged in a moment of shared stress were more likely to get physical sooner than other relationships – popped into his head.

'Officer Clag. Phoebe.' He took a deep breath. 'I feel that there's something I need to get off my chest.'

'Not right now, Misha.' whispered Phoebe. 'Someone's coming.'

There were more footsteps, but heavier than a hen's this time. A figure appeared, silhouetted in the doorway.

'Lights,' said the figure.

All the lights blazed on at once. Misha gasped. The figure in the doorway looked exactly like he imagined a space pirate would look: shiny, black, knee-length boots with silver lightning bolts on the tips, a half-unbuttoned shirt, a Byronic kind of haircut, a livid scar across his cheek and a dangerous-looking ray-gun hanging from his belt. Misha had a pretty generic imagination, as it turned out. He closed his eyes. Phoebe closed hers. Then she opened them again. Then she blinked a few times. Then she frowned.

'Hey, dollface,' said the figure.

Phoebe pocketed her truncheon and got to her feet. She shook her head. She heaved another big sigh. Finally, she groaned for good measure.

'Hello, Glen,' said Phoebe.

Chapter Seven

'What are the odds of that?' said Glen, for the fifth time. 'I mean, *what are the odds of that?*'

'Yes, low,' said Phoebe. 'I think we already agreed on this point.'

Glen laughed, stroked his floating ponytail thoughtfully, scratched a well-defined pec, and shook his head in continued disbelief. 'Sometimes, cupcake, it's like the universe is trying to tell us something.'

Misha sucked miserably on his coffee, and marvelled at how his life found exciting new ways to get worse. The real leather magno-chaises longues on which the three of them were sat hummed expensively. Not particularly tasteful wallpaper swirled, coalesced and melted away again on the walls of what he had now established as being Phoebe's ex-boyfriend's top of the range starship. The cabin's luxury chrome fittings glittered around him in a really annoying way.

'What are you even *doing* here, Glen? And why are you wearing that shirt?' Phoebe pointed to Glen's blousy shirt, which had a lot of ruffles on it. 'You look ridiculous.'

'I'm a pirate now! How great is that?'

'Oh, *Glen*, for crying out loud,' Phoebe threw her hands up in despair.

'Yeah, I guess you shouldn't be fraternising with me. But, in a way, doesn't that give this whole thing an extra frisson?' Glen flashed her an atomic white smile. 'I'm like the forbidden fruit that can never be.'

He spun his antique ray gun in the air in front of him and laughed again.

'Sorry about the waiting room, by the way. With the screams and the shrunken heads and all that stuff. It's mostly just to set the mood for visitors. The guy who designed the mural did my scar implant, too. Do you like it?' He pointed at the scar on his cheek. 'I'm wondering if I should get it moved a bit higher, have it go across the eyeball, maybe?'

'It's a very nice scar, Glen,' Phoebe said, politely. 'But I don't understand. I thought you were producing game shows on Alioth?'

Glen nodded. 'Yeah, I gave that a go for a while. Didn't work out. Had some disputes with the producers. I wanted goats behind the doors, they were saying it had to be spoons – because of some animal welfare nonsense – I wasn't prepared to compromise my artistic vision like that. So I went back to Lansbury Five, dabbled with millinery.'

'Hats?'

'Hats. I've always liked hats. But there's way too much politics with those people. Anyway, after *that* I moved into corporate promotional items. You know, stress balls, those pom-pom things with googly eyes; there's a real market for that stuff. But we had this warehouse fire – asteroids, jeez, asteroids are the *worst* – and so I took a sideways career move into Features Development on Phreetum Prime. I actually did pretty well at that – either of you guys see *Spacestation: Dogs*? About a space station run by dachshunds?'

Phoebe and Misha shook their heads.

'Well, you should check it out, the third act is mostly my direct input – point is, I was doing really great, the box office returns flowing in, but I wasn't *happy*, you know? I wasn't *fulfilled*. So I took a holiday to try to really … introspect. And one day, I'm sitting on the quartz beach near

Barnard's Star, and I look down, and I see this bug. He's looking right back at me, waving his little feelers. And we sort of shared this moment, this all-the-creatures-in-the-universe-connected-by-a-single-thread type of thing. And then a pigeon came and ate him. Just pecked his head right off. Powerful stuff. I had an epiphany right there. I realised that life is precious, you can be minding your own business alongside some guy with great cheekbones and a nice shirt, and then— Bam! You get eaten by a pigeon. It could happen to any one of us at any time. That was it for me, I went back to Features Development and I said, 'Dave,' – this was Dave Bendrix, head of the studio – 'Dave, I quit. You'll have to do *Target: Space Donkey* without me.'

Glen leaned back, the chaise longue gently adjusting its magnetic field to the contours of his body, and beamed. 'Best thing I ever did. Stepped out of the rat race. I don't get why everyone doesn't do it. Just quit their boring jobs today. What are those people thinking? It's weird.'

'Mmmm,' said Phoebe. 'How *is* your dad's real estate empire?'

'What? It's fine.' Glen frowned. 'I can't really see how that's relevant to the story at hand. Anyhow, I decided to live life on the edge. Occupy the moment. And now here I am, dashing space pirate.' He did an elaborate bow, got some of his sleeves' billowy ruffles caught in an air vent and took a moment to untangle himself. 'What do you think of the old girl?' he added, gesturing to the gleaming ship. 'I've christened her the *Lili Damita*, after the wife of famous historical buccaneer Errol Flynn, from back in the 17th century. She's a Zorgan Peterson Fer-de-lance RX1 limited edition. *Starships You People Can't Afford* magazine asked to do a spread on it.'

'It seems very clean. Like it hasn't had much action.'

'Well, I've only been in the game a couple of months. I've not done any actual pirating yet, per se. God, Pheebs, I forgot that you can be needlessly confrontational. It's a very unattractive trait. I think that might be why we split up.'

'We split up because you had sex with a ski instructor on Gordonworld.'

'Tomayto, tomarto. Do you like my hen?' said Glen, deftly changing the subject. He whistled, and the hen hopped up onto his lap.

'GAY,' said the hen.

'I don't think I do,' said Phoebe. 'What IS it?'

'It's a hen. A guy sold it me on the basis that apparently in the old times pirates used to walk about with hens attached to their shoulders.'

'I'm not sure that's right.'

'Well, no, I know that *now*.'

'NICE PINS,' said the hen. 'CALL THIS NEWS?'

'Sorry,' said Glen, flipping a switch on the hen's neck and pouring some birdseed into a pipette. 'It's been bio-engineered to talk. And there's some AI implanted in there too.'

'Artificial intelligence is very, very illegal, Glen.'

'Don't worry, I don't think it counts when it's this poorly implemented. Some college guys did an experiment by hooking a self-teaching AI program up to all the galaxy's newsfeeds, and implanted it into a hen. Except these boffins didn't stop to think about how ninety-nine percent of the intergalactic chatter is just *comment sections*, right? So the thing has precisely learnt to emulate the type of people that comment on news stories. The upside is I got her pretty cheap.'

'GIRLS DON'T GET GAMING,' said the hen.

'The downside is she's an idiot.'

Phoebe rubbed her temples. Conversations with Glen had always given her a bit of a headache. 'Your career history and your pirate hen are very interesting, obviously, but really I meant: what were you doing HERE. At this exact spot in space. Rescuing us.'

'Oh, right, yeah, got you. Well, see, there's a hidden message board you won't know about, because it's a criminal underworld thing.'

Phoebe rolled her eyes. 'We know about the message boards, Glen.'

'Really?' momentarily, Glen looked disappointed. 'Okay, anyway, the other day there's this bounty pops up. It's for a ship leaving the *Jim Bergerac*. And I thought to myself, hey, why do I know that name? Then it hit me – that's where Phoebe works now! So I figured I'd kill two birds with one stone. Kill in a literal sense, by turning up and collecting the ransom on your man here, and in a less literal sense, by getting the chance to see you again, babe. I like what you've done with your hair.'

'Glen, you can't just murder people. That isn't a socially acceptable occupation. And I thought you said you were a pirate, not an assassin.'

'It's all in that same general outlaw milieu, isn't it? I guess you get to wear a lot of black in the hit-man business, that's the appeal of that side of things. I look good in black. But I don't really fancy going on one of those voyages of self-discovery hit-men are always having. Meaningful life lessons don't sit well with me. Bit academic now. I stopped off at a services for that second cheese scone and this mysterious dude who attacked you must have beaten me to the punch by a couple of minutes. Kind of lucky for you how it worked out though.'

'Okay,' said Phoebe, the police bit of her brain taking over for a moment. 'So, you're telling me someone put a bounty on Misha's ship?'

'Now, see, that struck me as odd too,' said Glen. 'Who's going to go to the effort of offing some harmless schlub – no offence, guy –' he grinned at Misha, who went on staring miserably at his coffee, '– in a transport barn? I figured he had to be shifting something better than pigs.'

Phoebe and Misha both looked at the vibrating Lenslok box.

'I suppose somebody really doesn't want somebody else to get whatever is inside this box,' said Misha.

'What's in it?' asked Glen, taking a bite out of an apple and flexing a bit.

'No way of knowing,' said Phoebe. 'It's Lensloked, so we can't open it without the decoder. Impossible to break a Lenslok, everyone knows that.'

'Can't we just hack it open? With a brick or something?'

'We could, but it's going to detect that, and automatically fry whatever is in there, which doesn't do us much good.'

'So what then?'

'Well, first I can check to see what's on my crime scene recorder.' She tapped her head. 'Can I use this?' she said, pointing at a computer terminal.

'Be my guest.'

Phoebe uploaded the contents of her automatic black box implant with a waggle of her eyebrow. 'Okay, let's see what we've got.'

A stereoscopic Phoebe's eye view of Misha in the nightclub filled the screen.

'Yes,' he was saying, *'so another great thing about being a successful galactic trader is the views.'*

Misha reddened, and Phoebe quickly hit fast-forward. It got to the bit where the mysterious silvery ship turned up.

'No markings, no ID trace. Someone a bit more professional than you, Glen. But let's see what we've got on spectroscopy.'

The computer whizzed through the list of elements and compounds recorded at the moment of the attack, looking for a chemical fingerprint, like a telltale type of mud on the sole of a burglar's shoe, but drew a blank.

Phoebe sighed. 'Okay, that just leaves us with the original message putting the bounty on Misha. Let's have a look at it.'

Glen shook his head. 'It's a pirate trade secret. There's an outlaw code of honour. I don't think I should be sharing it with you.'

'Glen.'

Glen pouted, but logged on to the network. A screen popped up. The words 'WELCOME TO PONY MAGIC: FRIENDSHIP IS SUPER discussion forum' flashed in bright pink letters.

'Pony magic?' said Misha, feeling out of his depth.

'It's an old terrorist trick,' explained Phoebe. 'To avoid drawing attention to yourself you leave messages on an innocuous-looking forum.'

'It's not *just* that,' said Glen. 'A lot of us pirates are quite into Pony Magic. I think we like it *ironically*, but to be honest I've kind of lost track. Anyway, there you go,' he pointed to the message. 'It was from Sparklechops17. A set of coordinates, this guy's flight ID, and an account number. The usual stuff.'

'The trouble is,' said Phoebe, slumping back in her chaise longue, 'There's no way of tracing Sparklechops17 with these things. Everything gets routed through out-of-system tax haven bank accounts. Sparklechops17 wires the money to a holding account, verified by a third party; the successful assassin receives the cash upon providing evidence of the hit. They never have to deal directly with each other at all. Except …' Phoebe paused, trying to remember something. 'Except I think I've heard of Sparklechops17 before somewhere.'

'Sparklechops is one of the main ponies, probably you're just thinking of that,' said Glen. Phoebe looked at him. He shrugged. 'Seriously, it's a good show; it has well-thought-out themes.'

Phoebe shook her head again, logged into the police database, and started to scroll through some news files. Glen yawned, and spun his couch round to face Misha.

'So, you're from Gippsworld, right?'

Misha nodded.

'Pretty happening indigenous art scene going on down there. You involved in that?'

'No, not really.'

'Shame. I think art is what makes us human, don't you? I mean, that and thumbs.'

'Absolutely,' said Misha.

'There, look − Sparklechops17!' Phoebe jumped up so fast she detached from the chaise longue's magnetic field and had to clamber back down again. 'I knew it! I knew I'd seen it before. It was Sparklechops17 who put a bounty on Cliff Ganymede. The idiot didn't bother setting up a different account.'

'So what does that mean?' said Glen.

'It means that whatever is inside that case has something to do with the *murder of Cliff Ganymede*.' She grinned, because this time she wouldn't be turning up to Peterson's office with some tenuous missing-cargo non-event, she'd be turning up with a genuine Exciting New Lead. 'Come on, we've got to get this back to the station.'

'Whoa, hold up there,' said Glen.

'What?'

'Sorry, Pheebs, but nothing doing.' Glen shook his head firmly. 'As a paid-up member of the pirating fraternity, I can't be seen delivering criminals, even harmless schlubs – again, no offence – to *police stations*. I've got a reputation to maintain. It would not fit with my personal brand.'

Phoebe opened her mouth to say something, but then stopped. She thought about things for a moment and chewed her lip. She didn't care very much about Glen's personal brand. But she also didn't want to just desert Misha to his second-rate-criminal fate. And, more than anything, she couldn't bear the thought of having to hand over her big new discovery to Alicia. She could already see her doing that patronising, low-wattage smile of her. *We'll take this from here. You've done a very good job. Best leave it to the professionals now.'* Besides which, Phoebe reasoned, if you wanted to get *technical* about it then really neither Misha nor Glen had done anything particularly illegal so far. Until they found out what was inside the Lenslok box, Misha wasn't guilty of smuggling. And if Glen's concentration span was like she remembered he would probably have got over his piracy fad by the start of next week.

Phoebe stopped chewing her lip and sat up straight. She had come to a decision.

'Okay – here's the deal,' she said. 'I've got some leave saved up. I'm going to call the station, let them know I've decided to take a few days off. My boss was on about me working too hard, anyway.'

'So you're not going to turn me in?' said Misha.

'Not yet. Not until we know what's in that box, at any rate.'

'Won't you have to explain about your ship getting blown up?'

81

'I'll tell them it's in the garage getting an ammonia leak fixed. They won't notice for ages. Our division's administrative record-keeping isn't the best.'

'I'm confused,' said Glen. 'Because I stopped listening. What's happening, exactly?'

'I'll tell you what's happening,' said Phoebe, giving the Lenslok box a resolute thump. 'We're going to solve the Cliff Ganymede case ourselves, get my career back on track, and show those homicide division gits who's proper police.'

'What's in it for me?' said Glen.

'It's a chance to make up for your wicked pirate ways?'

'I'm not keen.'

'Please, Glen, this is *important*.'

'Tell you what,' said Glen, rubbing his chin. 'I'll help out if we can agree to forget the, frankly pointless, details of who said what to who or which one of us had sex with which ski instructor, and you'll let me take you to dinner.'

'I don't think that's a great idea.'

'Deal-breaker.'

Phoebe rolled her eyes and decided to cut her losses. 'Fine. Once we're done, I'll let you take me out to dinner. One dinner.'

Misha's shoulders somehow managed to slump even further than they already had done.

'Well then.' Glen poured out some SynBrandy, and bubbles of it floated across the cabin. 'To the new crime-busting gang! Phoebe, Glen and – what was your name again?'

'Misha.'

'Yeah, Phoebe, Glen and Maurice. Muzzletov!'

'YOUR ALL DICKS,' said the hen.

'Sorry,' said Glen, 'I accidentally nudged the switch back on.'

Chapter Eight

'How do we actually *do* it? Solve the murder, I mean?' said Misha, after they'd finished toasting their impending success for a moment.

Phoebe stopped feeling quite so upbeat. She hadn't ever worked a homicide investigation. Police training, before you specialised, was limited to the basics. The best way to accept bribes. Proper procedure for carrying out an effective frame-up. How to obscure your ID signal during a riot so you couldn't be identified if you got a bit too zealous with the ion cannon. The usual day-to-day bits and bobs. But she'd read enough pulpy detective fiction during her department's interminable personal development seminars to be hopeful that Ganymede's murder would involve a couple of gigantic, easy-to-spot contrivances, like killer twins, or a code carved onto the back of a turtle, or a rare bee.

'Well,' said Phoebe, doing her best to sound like she knew what she was talking about, 'The first step is always to talk to the last people to see the victim alive. Nine times out of ten the murder was done by the person who found the body. Wasn't that his agent?'

'Recently fired ex-agent,' said Glen, scrolling through an old news report.

'So there's your motive,' said Misha, keen to join in and show off his grasp of police terminology.

Glen tapped some more stuff into the computer. 'Marty

Zeevon. Let's see where Marty is … ah, bingo. He's making an appearance at something called GanyCon.'

'What's GanyCon?' said Phoebe.

Glen pointed to the screen.

'"The system's premier Cliff Ganymede Fan Cruise",' he read out loud. '"The GanyCon cruise has now been running continuously for sixty years aboard the luxury liner *President Lindsay Lohan*, and offers fans of Cliff Ganymede's books, games and long-running show the chance to buy merchandise, mingle with the stars of *Galloping Ganymede!*, attend inspiration workshops, discussion panels and, until his recent untimely death, listen to Cliff himself give motivational talks." Here, look, there's an online brochure.'

'"Marty Zeevon In Person – Remembering my time with Cliff",' read Phoebe, scanning through the events page. She looked at her watch. 'He's on tonight. Can we get there in time? Does this thing have hyperspace?'

'It's an *RX1*. It has hyperspace coming out the wazoo,' said Glen, typing in the coordinates, and flipping a switch to power up the drive plant.

'I can't believe we're going to GanyCon!' said Misha, perking up a bit. 'I've always wanted to see it. I heard they had a life-size statue of Cliff built out of rare collectible soaps.'

Glen arched an eyebrow. 'Are you a *fan*, Misha?'

Misha realised Phoebe was staring at him, and tried to look a bit less excited. 'Well, I mean, I've read the books. I watch the show. I wouldn't necessarily say I was a *fan*. I've got two, maybe three resin dioramas.'

'Of course, it's a non-docking independent ship, so I have no jurisdiction there,' said Phoebe, reading through some more of the brochure. 'We'll just have to hope they're nice people.'

'They've been on a *fan cruise* for sixty *years*,' said Misha, 'They'll be the nicest people in the galaxy!'

* * *

The hyperspace jump was worst for Misha, because he was new to it and so hadn't known what to expect.

'Oh god,' he said, holding his head in his hands as the universe folded and unfolded itself like a really big, boring piece of origami, almost instantaneously popping them out at their destination.

'Don't worry,' said Phoebe, giving him a consoling pat on the shoulder. 'That sensation of total self-awareness and of seeing your entire life in the third person goes away after a few seconds.'

'You know, I never get that,' said Glen. 'Maybe I'm already *too* self-aware.'

'I don't think it's that,' said Phoebe.

'HEN IS HORRIFIC,' said the hen, a single avian tear dropping from its beady eye.

The *President Lindsay Lohan*, in lazy orbit around the boiling magenta surface of Jodrell Three, filled up most of the observation window now. She was large enough to take up an entire double-page spread in the *Gollancz Bumper Book of Space Going Vessels*. According to the blurb, she had six spas, a steam room, five restaurants – including one run by a celebrity chef – and a contemporary décor that demonstrated 'a love for elegance and a passion for today's modern lifestyle'. She could even boast onboard gravity, thanks to the spinning circular deck set into the middle of the giant trapezoid hull. As they coasted towards her, Misha was irritated to see that, even though the *Lili Damita* had a perfectly good docking computer, Glen insisted on flicking the settings over to manual, and proceeded to slide into a parking spot with textbook ease. 'Smooth like substitute nutrient paste,' said Glen, winking at Phoebe, who just stared at her nails and turned a bit red.

* * *

'I hope they validate.' Glen examined his ticket stub as they rode the lift from the parking terminal up to the ships' arrivals lounge. 'Ten credits for a half-hour stay? And they call *me* a pirate.'

'Nobody calls you a pirate, Glen,' said Phoebe, with a sigh.

'Clean clothes are fun clothes, Phoebe Clag,' chirped the lift's automatic advertising system. 'Laundry facilities available on level two.'

'One weird trick to increase girth, Misha Bulgakov,' it added, after another quick body-scan.

'We should start taking the stairs,' said Misha, glowering at the holo-fac display.

* * *

A stately rotating hologram of Cliff Ganymede's head stared down at them from the middle of the chintzy lounge, messages of condolence scrolling through the air beneath it. A couple of bored bellhops loitered by the ticket desk. Various props and pieces of *Galloping Ganymede!* memorabilia were dotted about the place.

'Oh, wow, look at this,' said Misha, pointing to a big fibre-glass egg looming by some baggage trolleys. 'It's the Roc egg from season three, episode six, "You Can't Fry A Hyper-Omelette Without Breaking Free From Self Doubt". And here's the Cup of Creative Empowerment from season nine!'

'So what's the deal with this Cliff Ganymede guy, anyway?' said Glen. 'Why's he so popular?'

'He was the first person to really try to meld the two genres of "self-help" and "spaceport thriller",' said Misha enthusiastically. 'It's actually a brilliant idea – you get to transform your drab life into something much more dynamic and goal-orientated, whilst at the same time reading about Thargoid invasions and smuggled narcotics.'

'Sounds dumb,' said Glen. 'You know what's a good TV show? That one where they do surgery to make people look like zoo animals.'

'Hi,' said Phoebe, walking up to the ticket desk. 'Three tickets to the Ganymede convention, please.'

The man behind the desk laughed. Then he looked apologetic when they didn't laugh along with him. 'I'm sorry, I thought you were doing a funny joke. The convention is sold out. There's a twelve-year waiting list.'

'The thing is,' Phoebe leant forward, and dropped her voice to a whisper, 'we're here to investigate a murder.'

'Sorry,' said the man again, as unmoved as if he heard that six times a day. 'Perhaps you'd be interested in one of the other events? Are any of you in plastics? There's a plastics symposium on deck three. Or, if you're fans of Zargella Lombard, the movie star, she's doing a cabaret this evening. I hear there's an amazing bit where she duets with one of the singing civets of Proxima Five. It's actually a very cruel process because the "singing" is just a side effect of their unsuccessfully trying to digest Lavian gin berries. That's what makes it so brilliant. Your hen would get in half-price, by the way.'

Phoebe pouted. She hadn't been expecting to fall down at the very first hurdle. 'This sort of shit never happened to the Three Investigators,' she said, scowling.

'Do you think we could break in?' suggested Misha, trying to be helpful.

87

'I don't fancy our chances much.' She jabbed a thumb towards where a security robot with a laser for a face bobbled about near the doors.

'Leave this to the G-Dog,' said Glen, cricking his neck, and striding over to a small crowd of people standing behind a velvet rope. They were all holding up little signs, waiting for recent arrivals.

One of the signs had 'Cliff Ganymede Theatre Troop' written on it. It was being held up by a girl in a T-shirt emblazoned with the slogan 'BE AN AUTHENTIC LEADER, NOT A THARGOID CLONE'.

Glen walked straight up to her, and stuck his hand out. 'Hi there,' he said.

'Are you with the theatre troop?' said the T-shirt girl, looking him up and down.

'Yes, we are. Theatre. Greasepaint. Roar of the crowd. All that stuff. I'm riddled with neuroses, because I'm an actor, and she's quite easy,' he pointed to Phoebe, 'because she's an actress. And this guy's here too for some reason.'

'Oh! Well, what a relief!' the girl beamed. 'You're even slightly early.'

'Yeah, about that,' Glen sauntered back to the ticket desk. He leaned over and read the man's name-badge. 'Hey, Dan. There's a chance another lot will turn up here claiming to be the *real* theatre troop, but they are, of course, impostors.'

'Impostors?'

'Terrorists,' whispered Glen conspiratorially. 'You should neutralise them before they have a chance to activate their exploding shoes, or whatever it is they use these days. Aim for the head.'

'Thanks,' said the ticket booth man, smiling. 'I'll let security know to be on the lookout.'

'I like your hen – is that an actor thing?' said the girl, ushering them towards the big double doors at the far end of the arrivals lounge. 'I'm Denise, by the way, society treasurer, and I'll be looking after you. Actually, I don't want to boast, but this performance was my idea.'

'Well, it was a *great* idea, Denise,' Glen fixed her with the full-beam of his grin. Denise blushed, swiped an ID at the security bots and took a deep breath. At the same time she pulled a pistol from her belt and flicked off the safety.

'Can't be too careful,' she said, with a grimace. 'Stay close, just in case.'

They stepped inside a vaulted function room, built on such a gigantic scale that it made everyone feel as if they'd been hit by some kind of impossible shrink-ray. Aside from the size, though, it was kind of disappointing. If the décor had maybe once demonstrated a passion for elegance and today's modern lifestyle, it now looked, to Misha's dismay, as if all it was demonstrating was a passion for bloodstains and bullet holes. There were lots of stalls and merchandise booths, but most of them were on fire. The statue built out of collectible soaps was half melted. A few hollow-eyed convention goers loitered around, buying hats and band-aging wounds, but they all seemed twitchy and shell-shocked. There were evil-looking scorch marks all over the place. It smelled of explosive and discharged plasma rifles and death.

'There are more corpses than I'd expected on a fan cruise,' said Phoebe, nervously looking at a big stack of body bags piled up in one corner.

'Sorry,' said Denise. 'Somebody should have put those in the incinerator by now. It's been a difficult time, as you can imagine. I can't tell you how important it is that this evening's performance goes well,' she added, guiding them through the smoking wreckage. 'The peace treaty was only signed last week, so things are still pretty fragile.'

'Peace treaty?' repeated Phoebe, confused.

'I'm afraid the shipping wars have been going on for as long as anyone can remember,' said Denise with a nod, as if that explained everything. 'But it's so exciting to have you here! We could have just used avatars, I know a lot of people say you can't even tell the difference nowadays, but I think it's so much better to use actual actors. You can't fake the twinkle in the human eye, can you? I just know that you're really going to bring the piece alive. Obviously when Cliff died so unexpectedly we were robbed rather of a *Galloping Ganymede!* season finale, so the hope is that this enactment of what it might have been like will help bring about a much needed sense of closure for everyone.'

A small gaggle of fans inched in their direction, but Denise shot a warning stun blast above their heads and they backed away. She swiped the trio through another door. 'Right, this is your dressing room. The show doesn't get going for another two hours, so you've got a bit of time to relax.' She frowned, suddenly noticing something. 'Where are your costumes?'

'We had some trouble on the way over,' Glen rolled his eyes. 'Asteroids. Bloody asteroids, man, am I right?'

'Oh well, I suppose that shouldn't be a problem, it's not like there's a shortage of the stuff around here. I'll have some delivered to you. Who is playing who? No, wait, let me work it out. Obviously, you must be Princess Francine, because she's the woman one–' Denise nodded at Phoebe – 'and of course you must be "Clive" Ganymede, that goes without saying, because of your easy charm and toned musculature.' She grinned at Glen. 'So I suppose you must be Skrag? Ganymede's ratty, but well-meaning, half Thargoid ward-come-butler?'

Misha pulled a face. 'Yes, that's me, I guess.'

'I've got to check on a delivery of commemorative plates. Anything you need before I go?'

'As it happens, there is, Denise. We were hoping we might get a chance to have a quick word with Marty Zeevon?' said Phoebe.

'Why do you want to talk to Mister Zeevon?'

'Actor stuff,' said Glen. 'I think speaking to someone who actually *knew* Cliff would really help me inhabit the character.'

'Of course! But I'm sorry, Mister Zeevon won't be arriving until the after-show party. You'll be able to see him then. He'll be doing a signing along with the talk. So, anyhow, hope you break a leg tonight! Is that what we're meant to say?' Denise smiled apologetically at Phoebe. 'That wasn't supposed to be a reference to your freakish cybernetic limb by the way.'

She gave them a cheery wave and disappeared back into the hall. Phoebe slumped onto a couch.

'Well, that was weird,' she said.

'This isn't how it looked in the brochure *at all*,' agreed Misha. 'What was that stuff about shipping wars? Why would a *pleasure cruise* get involved in a trade dispute over galactic *shipping lanes*?'

'No, you're right, it doesn't make much sense,' said Phoebe, rifling through a complimentary fruit-basket. 'Perhaps it's *not* just a pleasure cruise? Maybe they've been transporting a bit of cargo on the side? Wouldn't be the first time. And traders can get pretty uppity about people messing with their territory. But, anyhow, I don't think that's our pressing concern. Our pressing concern is that we're busted.'

'We're not busted, we're fine,' said Glen. He pointed to the wall where a big motivational poster of Cliff Ganymede punching a polar bear pulsed gently. The bear had the word 'doubts' written on his side. 'Stop being so negative. Take a leaf out of Cliff's book.'

'But you heard Denise,' said Phoebe. 'Zeevon isn't around until after the performance. By which time our cover is blown. I mean, let's face it – we can't actually go out there and put on a show.'

'Sure we can,' said Glen. He grinned at Misha. 'Maurice here knows this stuff backwards. Come on, Maurice, you can write us a script. How hard could it be?'

'Well, I suppose …' Misha scratched the back of his neck and thought for a moment. 'The *Galloping Ganymede!* episodes *are* pretty schematic. Just about every week some familiar household object threatens the entire galaxy. Then Cliff and his crime-fighting partner, Skrag, a half human/half Thargoid butler, investigate. Nine times out of ten it turns out the beautiful but diabolical Princess Francine is behind it all along. Usually Skrag has a crisis of confidence, but Cliff uses some of his self-help advice to talk him round. Then there's a heartwarming bit where they laugh at something or other and Cliff gives out a healthy recipe.'

'You've got two hours. Think you can do it?'

Misha looked at Phoebe, who was looking back at him almost hopefully. The poster on the wall dissolved into a new image, this one showing Cliff riding a horse with 'positive thinking' painted on its flank.

'Yes, I can,' said Misha, manfully.

* * *

'Okay, you're on in ten,' said Denise, popping her head round the door and giving them a thumbs up. 'The club president is going to give a quick introduction, and then it's straight into you guys.'

She disappeared out the door again. Phoebe tugged at the hem of her skirt. 'I feel ridiculous.'

'It looks good,' said Misha, trying not to stare.

'This "Princess Francine". I take it she's a space sex-worker, right?'

'No, she's a strong, independent woman who doesn't take any nonsense from the men in her life.'

'But chooses to wear an outfit with a boob window?'

'Women aren't the strong point of the Ganymede universe.'

'Well, I look *amazing*,' said Glen, stepping out from his changing room. He was clad head to toe in black PVC leatherette, dotted with silver studs, a couple of bright white stripes running down the arms. Misha was irritated to admit it, but Glen actually made a pretty convincing young Cliff Ganymede. He just had a natural sort of swagger to him.

* * *

The audience sat in two groups on either side of the vast hall. They eyed each other suspiciously, and pointedly fingered their ray guns and baseball bats and shivs and lengths of lead piping. The President of the Cliff Ganymede appreciation society, who turned out to be Denise wearing a different badge, stepped onto the stage and cleared her throat.

'Fellow fans, it has been a difficult time. The shipping war has taken its toll on all of us. But Cliff didn't die for nothing. The shock of his passing has brought us together. We have put our differences aside, and with the signing of our peace treaty the nightmare of the last sixty years is finally behind us. To celebrate this momentous occasion we've got a fun evening of entertainments lined up. Starting with a specially commissioned live performance of the never-filmed season finale, *Galloping Ganymede!: An Appointment with Explosions*. Please put your hands together for the award-winning Alioth travelling theatre ensemble.'

She took her seat in the audience, and gave Glen, Misha and Phoebe, waiting in the wings, an encouraging wink.

The lights dimmed and Glen's hen waddled out into the middle of the stage, illuminated by a single spot.

'EXT. THE SNOWY WASTES OF BIDMEAD SIX – EVENING,' said the hen, who had been switched over to her audiobook setting. 'GANYMEDE and SKRAG approach MASLOW'S PYRAMID OF NEEDS.'

* * *

Twenty minutes into the performance and Misha thought things were going pretty well. The audience wasn't the most attentive, and there'd been a slow section in the middle of Act Two where he could sense that he'd started to lose them a bit, but the surprise appearance of the mecha-crows from season four had seemed to prove popular. All they had to do now was get through the exciting third-act climax and they were home and dry.

'Finally we are here, Skrag,' said Glen/Cliff/Clive, reading the script that Misha had beamed to all of their retina displays. 'We have overcome challenges to our physiological wellbeing, our employment, our sexual intimacy and our self-esteem, and now, via this ventilation duct, we have arrived at the summit of this infernal pyramid – the chamber of self-actualisation.'

'CLIVE approaches the ZETA DEVICE,' said the hen. Glen picked up a slightly melted lunchbox that Misha had found on one of the merchandise stalls.

94

'Here it is. The Zeta Device, hidden by the nefarious Count Maslow a thousand years ago. A weapon of near infinite power. One simple press of a button and I can destroy the Thargoid race forever.'

'But Clive, do we have that right?' said Misha/Skrag, doing his best to project all the way to the back of the auditorium, because this was an important bit. 'The Thargoids are a terrible, warmongering race, but even so – to wipe out an entire species?'

'Foolish, flabby-minded Skrag, what have I told you?' said Glen. He ad-libbed by cuffing Misha around the head. 'You're *entitled* to the things you want. By asking "Do I have the right to commit genocide?" you're falling into the trap of Negative Thoughts. Haven't you been doing your exercises? Every morning: you look in that mirror and you tell yourself, "Not only CAN I wipe out the Thargoids, I DESERVE to wipe out the Thargoids, because I'm a great guy and I'm going places."'

Glen/Clive opened the lunchbox/Zeta Device. 'But what's this? The Zeta Device has gone! There is just a note. A note written in the all too familiar bubble writing of my nemesis.'

'A chill WIND blows through the CHAMBER, shadows play across the walls like the dancing spirits of yesteryear,' said the hen. Misha, pretty proud of that line, cast a quick glance towards the audience to see if they were impressed.

Phoebe walked on from the wings, still tugging at her skirt. There were a couple of half-hearted wolf whistles from the crowd. Phoebe glowered and gave them the finger. 'That's right, Clive,' she said to Glen, 'I – diabolical Princess Francine – already have the Zeta device here in my sexy hands.'

There was a tense pause. Phoebe looked questioningly at Misha, mouthed something, then focused on the script scrolling along her retina display. 'Oh, is it me again? Sorry. Tell me, Clive Ganymede, how did you escape my procrastination bees?'

'A simple case of neuro-linguistic programming,' said Glen. 'I employed the same positive reinforcement that I would use to convince a potential employer of my inherent dynamism, except I used body language rather than words. It's all in the shoulders. I soon had the bees eating out of my hand.'

'Your steady eye-contact and the way you've enhanced your personal credibility by building a strong social media presence certainly makes it difficult for me to best you,' said Phoebe. 'But over the years of our rivalry, I too have picked up some skills. You will recall, perhaps, that earlier in this adventure you stopped off at a bar, where you were offered a range of cocktails.'

'Another of your traps, Francine?'

'Indeed,' said Phoebe. 'For you see – I knew you would choose the blue Lavian gin, because blue is a colour associated with leadership and personal magnetism. But that gin was laced with a liquid explosive, milked from the teats of my Neptunian cows.'

'F/X: THERE IS THE SOUND OF EXPLODING INNARDS,' said the hen.

'What have you done, wretched slattern?' cried Glen. He made some groaning noises, and sank to his knees. Misha cradled him. Glen gurgled. 'I'm done for, faithful friend. Though I have conquered the twin evils of work-related anxiety and time management issues, even Clive Ganymede himself cannot conquer death. I never went to Alioth. I never went to Alioth.'

'That was really poignant, the way he said that twice, the second time slightly slower,' said Phoebe. 'Even though we were enemies, I shall miss you, Clive Ganymede.'

'You've killed him!' said Misha/Skrag.

He was pleased to hear the audience gasp at this news.

'I have. And now I will use the Zeta Device to fetroy the galaxy. Fetroy? Is that right?'

'I was having to type pretty fast,' whispered Misha with an apologetic shrug, before continuing in his 'projecting' voice. 'Do not do it, Francine. I sense good in you.'

'No, I am evil.'

'I don't think you're evil. I think you're just scared of being alone in the universe. You're searching for something to make you feel *connected*, and *whole*, and less *sad* – the same as all of us! And the truth is, you're not alone, Francine. For I, lowly Skrag, have a secret. I have been in love with you from afar for ages.'

Misha crossed over to her.

'I've never found the words to say it, but I have long hoped we might get together.'

He took Phoebe's hand. 'I would like you to be my Space Queen.'

Out the corner of his eye, Misha noticed that the supine audience weren't quite so supine anymore. There actually seemed to be a bit of a hubbub. People were shouting. He grinned at Phoebe. 'They're really into it. I think we've *moved* them. We should kiss.'

A plasma bolt skimmed past Misha's ear. Then a resin model of a Thargoid sailed through the air and smacked into the stage behind Glen. Misha looked more closely at the audience and realised that, rather than being on the edge of their seats, they were using them to try to stove each other's heads in.

'What on earth are you *doing*?' cried Denise, running on stage and laying down some covering fire as they both dived down behind a big prop rock.

97

'What's wrong? Why are they so upset?' said Misha. 'I realise the dialogue could have used a polish, but I don't think they should be this critical. Drama is hard.'

'The peace treaty!' said Denise, having to shout above the noise of the crowd and the sound of rifle blasts. 'You've ruined everything!'

'What are you talking about?' wailed Misha, as more plasma bolts knocked chunks of the wall away right above their heads. 'What's a stupid play got to do with a trade dispute?'

'Trade dispute? What trade dispute?'

'This shipping war you keep going on about.'

Denise stared at him like he was an idiot. 'Not a shipping war,' she hissed. 'A *shipping* war. A schism in the fandom with regards to which characters it was suitable to ship in Cliff Ganymede fan-fiction. It's the very *first* article of the peace treaty: The undersigned parties are agreed that at no point will they attempt to suggest romantic encounters between the characters of Gary Skrag and Princess Francine, because Skrag would be implausibly punching above his weight.'

An explosion rocked the room. People screamed.

'Fantastic,' said Denise. 'You've started a massacre.'

Another volley of bright yellow laser bolts took down the hall's chandelier and vaporised the remains of the soap statue. Molten chunks of metal rained down on the stage. Misha decided that theatre wasn't really in his blood.

In the midst of it all both he and Phoebe were surprised to see Glen calmly getting to his feet. He put his hands on his hips and whistled.

'Hey! Keep your *knickers* on,' said Glen, frowning at the audience. 'The show's not over yet. IT'S NOT OVER.'

The crowd took a second out from firing lasers at each other's faces, and turned to look at the stage again.

'That's right,' said Glen, adopting a heroic sort of pose. 'For you see – Clive Ganymede lives!'

Very slowly, the audience holstered their pistols, stopped waggling their bits of lead piping, and sat back down on the seats that weren't already on fire.

'Fair enough, let's see where this is going,' said one of the attendees. 'As fans, we're nothing if not reasonable.'

'I suppose we owe it both to the artistic process and to our own well-developed sense of perspective to reserve judgement,' said another, 'but there had better be a good twist ending.'

'Just follow my lead,' whispered Glen to Phoebe and Misha.

'INT. YOUR MOTHER'S BOUDOIR,' said the hen, who wasn't very good at improv. Phoebe quickly punted it behind the curtain. Glen strutted to the front of the stage.

'I knew Francine would be up to her treacherous ways, all women being inherently untrustworthy. So I made sure I took an antidote earlier in the day. Unfortunately, I cannot say the same for my weaselly side-kick, Skrag, who also drank the poisoned gin. It obviously has taken a bit longer for him to digest because of his awful mutant guts. Nonetheless, the Neptunian milk should be kicking in just about now, exploding him from the inside out in a horrific and painful way.'

Misha stared at Glen. Phoebe nudged him in the ribs.

'Ack!' said Misha. 'My intestines!' Then he made a show of clutching his neck and flopping onto the floor.

Glen gave him a pitying tap with his foot, and grabbed Phoebe by the waist. 'Princess Francine, I think we both know that your constant attempts to destroy me and the galaxy have just been an extreme and showy form of negging.'

He leaned down and kissed Phoebe. Misha watched

miserably as she kissed him back. After about ten seconds the kiss was still going on, so Misha stopped acting dead and stood up. He coughed and waved at the audience.

'Okay, great, well, there you go everybody, that's the end of the performance,' he said.

The audience debated amongst themselves for a moment, but – seemingly satisfied with this new romantic pairing – they eventually gave a halting round of applause. There was some grumbling about the pacing, and about some glaring continuity issues, and about how Phoebe had pronounced the name of the planet 'Temabilis'. Most of them agreed that the hen was the best bit. 'A solid seven,' was the general consensus.

Denise hurried back on to the stage. 'Well, ladies and gentlemen, I hope you enjoyed that. An unusual interpretation of how the season finale might have gone, and one that inexplicably deviated quite radically from the script I provided some weeks ago.' She shot Misha a testy look. 'But a very entertaining way to kick off our evening, nonetheless. We've got the after-show party and Marty Zeevon himself in a little while, but first we'll be judging the baking competition to see who has managed to produce a show stopper loaf that most embodies the message from Cliff's penultimate book, *When Life Gives You Biomechanoid Bore-Slugs, Make Disgusting Bore-Slugade*.'

Chapter Nine

'Well, that was pretty intense,' said Glen, as they stood in the queue of fans waiting to get Marty Zeevon's signature. 'Nifty bit of writing there, Tolstoy.'

'Sorry,' said Misha, still trying to wipe off his stage makeup, worrying now that it was going to bring him out in one of his rashes. The line shuffled forward a few inches.

'You did really well, Misha,' said Phoebe, patting his shoulder. 'It wasn't your fault. I thought your script was actually quite moving.'

'And at least the G-Dog was there with some mad improvising skills,' said Glen. He made little pointy gun shapes with his hands and fired imaginary bullets at his own nipples.

'It was very brave, Glen, the way you just stood up like that. Those laser bolts going off all over the place. You could have been *killed*,' said Misha, with a wistful sigh, imagining for a fleeting, happy moment Glen's head exploding across the convention hall like a watermelon dropped off a pig silo.

Glen laughed, and looked slightly confused. 'Laser bolts? What are you talking about?'

Phoebe stared at him. 'They were *shooting* at us, Glen. How could you not have noticed that?'

'Jesus Christ, seriously? I just saw them lob a few figurines,' he rubbed his chin. 'Oh, man, I forgot – it'll be the eye surgery. I can't really see any bright colours. Had a guy in the Malpha system scrape most of the cones out from

101

my retinas. It's like *the* most hip procedure these days: gives everything a washed out, cinematic look. Makes it seem like you're in an independently produced movie all the time. You should try it.'

'Good grief.'

'By the way, pretty good "acting" on that kiss there, cupcake.'

'Well, that's what it was. Acting,' said Phoebe, shooting Misha a quick, anxious glance. 'Let's just be really clear on that.'

'Sure it was, Pheebs. Sure it was. You know, I think I might keep this costume when we're done.' Glen rubbed his square jaw and gazed appreciatively at his own reflection in one of the room's portholes. Then he looked at the fans ahead of them in the queue and rolled his eyes. 'Come on, losers, keep it moving along here.' He turned back to Phoebe and Misha with an exasperated shake of his head. 'Have you noticed how, despite what it says on the posters, nobody here really *looks* particularly dynamic and goal orientated?'

They finally got to the front of the queue. Marty Zeevon, looking like an impossibly wrinkled human walnut in thick pebble spectacles, peered myopically up at them from where he sat behind his desk, next to a big stack of glossy photographs. The photographs showed Marty with his arm around Cliff. It had obviously been taken a few decades before, because, wrinkle-wise, Marty looked less like a walnut, more like a pug.

'It's two credits a signature,' he rasped. 'Three, if you want it personalised in any way. If your name has more than six letters I charge an extra credit.'

'Mister Zeevon, we were hoping to talk to you about Cliff Ganymede's murder,' said Phoebe, deciding to cut straight to the point.

'It was a real shame – Cliff was a swell guy. Didn't they decide it was suicide? There – that's an extra credit for small talk.'

'Could we ask you a few questions? In private, perhaps?'

Marty nodded at his stack of ten by eights. 'I'm not going anywhere until I've got through this lot.'

'It won't take long.'

'No dice, honeybunch.'

'Look,' said Glen, taking out a very shiny credit card. 'What if we just bought all of these? Sign the whole lot to Maurice, he's a big fan.'

'All of them?' Zeevon narrowed his eyes for a moment. He sat back and folded his arms. 'If you want to talk, I'm going to need to eat.'

'Great. Let's do that.'

'You guys will pay for dinner?'

'Sure,' said Phoebe, keen to try to move things along.

'And I can have anything on the menu? The full menu, not the fixed thing – they give you smaller portions on the fixed thing.'

'Yeah, whatever.'

'Starters, cheese platter, the works?'

'*Fine.*'

'Hot-dog,' said Marty, breaking out into a grin. 'And they said old Marty Zeevon was washed up.'

* * *

'You know, I already talked to the cops,' said Zeevon, through a mouthful of Ganymede-themed self-worth burger and positivity fries. 'Nice girl. Alicia something.' He nodded at Phoebe. 'Your sort of age, but better conditioned hair.'

Phoebe smiled through slightly gritted teeth, and took a long drag on her Dynamism Root Beer. 'This is just a follow-up visit,' she explained. 'We're very thorough. Can you tell me about the last time you saw Cliff?'

'Not much to tell. He was on his book tour. I hadn't seen him for months, because by that point the guy was a virtual recluse. I don't exactly mean "wearing shoeboxes on his feet", but getting that way. At the half box/half shoe stage. So, when he sends me a message, suggests a drink, I'm surprised, you know? To be honest I should still be mad after he dumped me for Strickson, Sutton & Fielding, but what the hell, I figure: free drink. By the way, are you going to eat that?' he pointed at Glen's jacket potato.

'Be my guest,' said Glen, pushing it towards him.

'I get there, and I'm thinking maybe he wants to take me back. Not that I needed him. I've got a lot of great clients. People say Cliff was my one big client, and that I got lucky, but those people don't know what they're talking about. Where was I?'

'Seeing Cliff for the first time in months.'

'Right, so we met at this bar, same place he's staying – one of those upscale hotels with the name-brand hair products in the bathroom. Tip – when you check in to a place like that, you instantly hide the toiletries in your suitcase, and then call down to reception, like the cleaners just forgot to put them there in the first place. Double portions. Anyway – Cliff was pretty jumpy. He was moaning about his new publishers. That's what authors do, they *moan*, so I didn't really listen too closely. He said that he was having difficulties with them. Something about not being comfortable with the stuff they were trying to get him to do. The more he drank, the more paranoid the guy starts to sound. Shadowy forces out to get him, secret dossiers, the usual ravings. Honestly, I kind of drifted off. Things got cut short, because there was a bit of a scene.'

'What kind of a scene?'

'They had a fill-your-own plate salad bar. The baristabot got shirty about me building a tower to fit more food into, said it went against the spirit of the buffet. I say, if you provide a solid building block like parsnips you've got to expect a bit of architectural innovation – it's like they're penalising me for creativity. So we left and I took Cliff back to his room. He mumbled some stuff about having proof that would bring them all down, whoever "them" were, and that was the last time I spoke to him. When I came back the next morning to see why he hadn't shown for breakfast, I found the door ajar and Cliff out cold on the carpet.'

'Can you think of any significance the words "knuckle down" might have had?' asked Phoebe. 'He wrote that in his own blood, which is the sort of behaviour that usually constitutes a clue.'

'I figured it was a last message to his fans. Typical Cliff, telling everyone to work hard, when he was literally the laziest man you could ever meet.'

'Cliff Ganymede wasn't lazy!' Misha protested. 'He had harnessed his inner dynamo.'

Zeevon laughed. 'He was lazy. He was a lazy, lazy man. I never met anyone like him. I once saw the guy refresh a gossip site two hundred times in the space of an hour rather than actually type a sentence. He had twelve scheduled naps per day. You know, the only reason he even wrote his breakthrough book in the first place is because he had two commissions, a self-help book and a crime novel, and he thought by combining them he could get away with half the word-count.'

'I don't believe it,' said Misha, crossing his arms. 'He published hundreds of books. That's not lazy.'

'Procedural generation.'

'Pardon?'

'They were all procedurally generated. Computer games and movies have been using procedural generation for centuries, but it's still a bit frowned upon in the book world. That didn't stop Cliff, though. There was a list of about twenty phrases, and like a five-line algorithm. Didn't you ever notice that book-to-book they'd just give completely conflicting advice? So yeah, his usual working day was like this: set the computer going by six, it would have generated most of a book by six-oh-two. Then he'd spend the next hour and a half "adding the Ganymede magic", which basically meant he'd put in a few laboured beehive metaphors. Back in the day, back when he could still be vaguely bothered, he'd do other sorts of metaphor too, but in the end he felt bees were easiest.'

Misha nodded. 'For maximum productivity the working day should be structured like a beehive, with the legs in the morning, the main bit where the bees live in the afternoon, and the top part, the lid that stops the bees from flying off, that's the evening,' he recited.

'Goals are like honeycomb, hard to reach because they are surrounded by bees. Goals are hexagonal,' Marty sighed. 'He doesn't even bother to explain that one.'

Phoebe surreptitiously blinked on her Police Interview Facial Coding Polygraph. 'Mister Zeevon, we're in possession of a box. We think the contents are in some way linked to Cliff's murder. Do you have any idea what could be in there?'

'Sorry, not a clue.'

'And you yourself didn't have anything to do with Cliff's death?'

'I'm an upstanding citizen! I'm shocked you'd even suggest such a thing.'

'Perhaps you were upset Cliff had gone to a new agency?'

106

'I told you – I didn't need the guy. I've got lots of top-tier clients. You ever heard of the band I represent, the Asteroid Belts? They're great. They've got an amazing gimmick. They wear really big belts. That's what you need in this business, a nice gimmick.'

Phoebe sighed. The polygraph scan didn't show anything untoward. She was fairly certain Zeevon wasn't much of an agent, but he didn't seem like much of a murderer either.

'Where did Cliff live?' she asked. 'We couldn't find anything for him on the database.'

'Yeah, it's tricky. See, along with the moaning, and the laziness, and the unhealthy pallor, the other thing about authors is: they really hate paying taxes. So, after the first few million rolled in, he bought himself one of those Bernal Spheres. You spin them right, you can get pretty nice gravity going, almost like the proper stuff, better than living on a regular space station. Feels like you're outside on the inside, if that makes sense. He fixed a big hyperspace generator to the side of it, and set it to randomly jump around. Not totally random, obviously, he didn't want to end up anywhere *risky*. Not much point hiding your gold under the mattress so the governments can't get it if you're just going to get it thieved by pirates. But he had, I don't know, I guess a few dozen places round the galaxy he'd pop out on. A few days later, the whole place jumps to somewhere new. Overkill, if you ask me. A bit tin-foil hat.'

'Do you know where we could find it?'

'I've got an address for one of the spots it appears at, but it's just some coordinates out in deep space. The thing should turn up sooner or later, but you could be there ten minutes, you could be there a week. No way of telling.' Zeevon shrugged and emptied a little tray of condiments into his pockets. 'You'll need to pack some board games.'

107

Chapter Ten

Homicide investigation is not proving to be as seat-of-your-pants exciting as I assumed it would be. We've been here at the coordinates Zeevon gave us for two days now, but there's been no sign of Ganymede's fancy house turning up.

This morning something strange happened when I was eating my ninth pot of synthetic noodles. Obviously, like all embedded packaging characters, Chet Noodles is programmed to be chirpy to the point of psychosis, but today, when I asked him to tell me some facts about the SynNoodles Brand he refused to answer for a while. Finally, when I persisted, he said that, 'If you took all the noodles made in a year and laid them end to end, they'd stretch to the moon.' It sounded a bit boilerplate. I asked which moon. At that point he said, 'Oh, you know, one of them, does it matter?' I told him that wasn't much of an answer, but he didn't say anything after that. My relationship with the Chet Noodles interactive packaging mascot is the only one I've had that has lasted longer than six months, so I find this development worrying.

On that note, I still can't really tell if Misha likes me. Glen is easier to read, having 'accidentally' walked in on me showering three times now. He claims this spaceship doesn't have any locks because 'there shouldn't be borders between humans'.

To pass the time I am reading Cliff Ganymede's classic text, *'Rocket Pod Alpha: Destination Girls!'* in which he lists three main ways to get someone to like you.

1) Pepper your conversation with words that suggest dynamism and virility.
2) Emphasise the many things you have in common.
3) Identify your unique qualities, then show these off.

I think my unique qualities are:

I snore quite badly, even in zero gravity – which should be impossible, because the mucous membranes of the nose have no pressure on them.

I intend to learn that coding language by the end of next year.

I was going to write that novel.

As far as I can see, me and Phoebe have the following traits in common:

We both have very poor posture; neither of us have any tattoos; we both suffer from itchy skin rashes.

Phoebe Clag's Case Notes – 4.10.3300

Things are not going well.

Misha has taken to pointing out repeatedly how much I slouch. I suppose the 'romantic' eye dilation I observed in the bar must have been because of a pituitary disease after all. Feel I should probably inform him of this, but every time I'm about to bring the subject up he starts to draw attention to my eczema.

In addition to the pituitary disease, there is a chance he is suffering some neurological issues as his speech patterns have become oddly hard to follow. He keeps on dropping words like 'sap' and 'robust' and 'loamy' into his sentences, seemingly at random. I'm thinking frontal-lobe tumour, though maybe it is a delayed effect of our earlier oxygen starvation.

Noodle update: today, when I tried to engage the noodle packaging in conversation, Chet Noodles flat out told me that he thought I should start interacting with other anthropomorphised marketing mascots, and that my eating twelve pots a day was making him feel 'claustrophobic'.

Nothing on the Ganymede house front. Starting to think maybe Zeevon got the address wrong. To make matters worse, Glen has found that he has an acoustic guitar onboard. This is an unwelcome development.

Misha's Diary – 4.10.3300

Casually mentioned to Phoebe about my unusual snoring facility. She said she'd already noticed, which must be a good sign. Managed to get the words 'fruitful', 'uberous' and 'pulchritudinous' into a conversation about biscuits.

I have also made sure to implement another Cliff Ganymede trick, which is to make yourself appear magnanimous and big-spirited. I have done this by mentioning Glen's good points as often as possible, even though he is my love rival. I find this difficult, because Glen has few redeeming features, though he is not afraid to wear his hair unfashionably long and walk around without any clothes on, which I guess I grudgingly respect.

I still haven't called dad to let him know about the transport barn. I'm going to be on pig parasite removal duties for a month.

Possibly Misha has a crush on Glen? When we're alone he hardly ever fails to mention how well developed Glen's upper body is, and how he has 'nice hands'.

Maybe I've been too harsh, and should consider going out with Glen again. In the spirit of scientific enquiry, I've taken a leaf out of Charles Darwin's dating book and made a list of pros and cons.

Good things about Glen:

Glen has amazing teeth.

Glen does not seem to have issues with my posture.

Bad things about Glen:

Glen uses the word 'illegible' a lot, but he does not seem to know what it means.

Glen thinks a good money-making scheme would be to breed horses that look like celebrities. When I ask how that would work, he keeps talking about how he's a 'big picture' guy.

Glen repeatedly refers to the fact that him being a pirate and me being a police officer makes us like the 'Montezumas and the Capuchins'.

Other reasons to go out with Glen:

It would stop my mother sending me news stories about the latest developments in creepy biomechanical companions with realistic skin.

Today when I went to eat some noodles I found a note on the packaging from Chet Noodles informing me that he needed some space to get things straight in his head. He had left Fido Dido in his place. I am not a fan of Fido Dido.

It has occurred to me that these are not very professional case notes. I hope this damn thing turns up soon.

Chapter Eleven

Cliff Ganymede's former home popped out of hyperspace next to the *Lili Damita* just as Glen was halfway through performing his new self-penned song, *'I Smuggled Furs And Alloys To Xeaan, But You Smuggled Feelings Straight To My Heart'*. Both Phoebe and Misha made a show of trying to look disappointed that they wouldn't get to hear the remaining nine verses, and then hurriedly busied themselves getting ready for docking. They touched down on the outer landing pad with a blast of the retro-boosters, strapped on masks in case the atmospheric filters weren't working anymore, and rode an automated little monorail down through a hole in the sphere's metal crust.

'This guy must have sold a *lot* of books,' said Glen, whistling appreciatively as they stepped onto the tiny inside-out world. 'You know there's a five-year waiting list to get one of these things? I've never seen my dad get so mad with a shop assistant as when he realised he couldn't just buy one on the spot.'

A bucolic landscape of rivers and fields and trees rose up dizzyingly all around them. It covered the entire inner surface of the sphere, the only break a big set of mirrors running along the length of the equator, reflecting enough light in from the nearest star to give everything a warm late-afternoon glow. It made Misha feel sick.

'It's not right,' he said, looking up at where, instead of sky, the landscape arched around in a continuous loop. 'I don't like it at all.' Somewhere a babbling brook burbled. A colourful songbird swooped, and crashed right into his head.

'Yeah, it's a nightmare for birds. Watch out for that,' said Glen. 'The gravity dissipates away from the surface, and then gets stronger again. Messes them up.' He turned to the hen, who was peering out from a backpack. 'Don't try to fly off, hen.'

'Hens don't fly, Glen,' said Phoebe.

'Really?' Glen stared at his hen again. 'Why have you got wings? Why are animals so unfathomable?'

'Come on,' said Phoebe, pointing at a house that would have been on the horizon if there had been a horizon, which there wasn't. 'That must be his place over there.'

They started to trek across the field, hacking through lush, knotted alien vegetation. A few incredibly good-looking insects buzzed past them. Topiary cut into the shape of Old Masters gave off the relaxing smell of money. Cliff obviously hadn't spared any expense when it came to decking the place out. As Phoebe pushed on a little way ahead, Glen hung back and waited for Misha to catch up.

'She's a great girl,' said Glen, watching Phoebe go.

'Yes,' agreed Misha.

'Tell me, Maurice: do you ever feel that there's more to life than bedding an endless succession of glossy, lithe-limbed beauties?'

Misha made a non-committal grunting noise.

Glen nodded. 'I've been contemplating that a lot, recently. You know how it goes – you're out at a club, or at a film premiere, or at an exclusive hover-car dealership or some-place, and *yet another* impossibly hot, fawn-like nymph starts cracking on to you, and you chat for a while, and then, inevitably, half an hour later you end up back at her place, and you have this crazy, untrammelled hyper-sex. And then you're lying there, drenched in sweat, and she's asleep next to you, the sheets not quite covering her perfect, honey-coloured thighs, and you just find yourself wondering: is this *really* all there is? Isn't there *something* more significant than all these exhausting erotic encounters? I mean, we've all felt it, right?'

'Yes,' said Misha, biting his lip. 'I guess we have.'

'Exactly, you get what I'm talking about. But here's the thing: I think maybe Phoebe is the woman to save me from all that. I really think she could be the one.'

Misha didn't say anything. Another confused bird flew into his face.

* * *

They weren't really expecting to find anyone at home, but Phoebe rang the doorbell of Cliff's whitewashed neo-classical mansion just in case. To her surprise she heard a clopping sound and then a muffled voice from inside shouted, 'Coming! Hang on. Oh for pity's sake. Oh. Oh goddamn. Jesus.'

Finally, the door swung open and a horse in a satin dressing gown looked out at her.

'Hi. Can I help you?' said the horse.

'AN ABOMINATION! SCIENCE GONE MAD,' said the hen.

'You're one to talk.'

'Hi,' said Phoebe, who was starting to take unexpectedly chatty creatures in her stride now, even if she still found the entire concept slightly irritating. 'We're here about Cliff.'

'You'd better come in, then.'

* * *

114

The horse showed them through into a dining room which would have been delicately tasteful if it hadn't been for the huge murals of a semi-naked Cliff Ganymede in amorous clinches with giant, highly-muscled bees.

'Cliff really did like bees, didn't he?' said Phoebe, wide-eyed.

'Yes, sorry about those,' said the horse. 'I realise that they're a *bit much*. Help yourself to drinks, by the way. I'd fix you them myself, but we'd be here all day.' The horse nodded at his hooves and rolled his eyes. 'I'm Cliff's automated diary,' he went on. 'In case you were wondering.'

'Oh, of *course*, you're the next model up from my hen,' said Glen, patting him on the neck. 'I read about these. It's really nifty. Wherever you are in the universe, a wireless link downloads all your experiences into your diary's genetically augmented brain. You can get it implanted in cats, dogs, dolphins. Never seen a horse version before.'

'The speech augmentation is very tricky with horses,' explained the horse. 'It's some very pricey vivisection.'

Phoebe rubbed her chin thoughtfully. 'So – you've got all of Cliff's memories?'

'That's right,' said the horse. 'To all intents and purposes I have lived all the things Cliff lived, known all the things he knew. I can also sync up to his appointment calendar and download financial spreadsheets.'

The horse tried awkwardly to sit down in a big, leather-backed armchair, then attempted to pull a cigar from his dressing gown. He instantly dropped the cigar on the floor and groaned.

'Bloody hell,' he said. Phoebe went over, picked the cigar up, put it in the horse's mouth and lit it for him.

'Thank you, my dear,' said the horse, puffing out a smoke ring. 'I've been *gasping*. So, anyway, are you friends of Cliff's?

I don't recall you from any of the memory dumps. But then, I haven't downloaded any updates for over a couple of months now. I'm beginning to think something might have happened to him. He was due back from the book tour ages ago.'

'You don't know?'

'Know what?'

Phoebe started to say something, but then changed her mind. She couldn't quite bring herself to break it to him.

'You've just been here, alone, waiting for him? Why didn't you try to raise the alarm?'

'I'm a horse. I don't contain any artificial intelligence. I just record Cliff's memories. I mean, I *say* I'm just a horse. There's some brain/CPU leakage, obviously. I've developed a taste for these cigars and some of the finer whiskeys. Or rather, I would have done, if I could ever get the tops off the bottles.' The horse did a whinnying sigh. 'You people, with your hands, you don't know you're born.'

'Listen, horse,' said Phoebe, gently. 'Could you maybe help us with a few questions?'

'I'll certainly do my best.'

'Do you have any idea what the significance might be of the phrase "knuckle down"?'

'Oh dear. Yes. I was afraid it might be something to do with this,' the horse puffed on his cigar and gazed out of the window. 'Poor Cliff, I'd rather hoped he *was* just being paranoid. You see, a little while back he moved publishers. Looking for a new stable, you could say, if you'll excuse my horse-based humour. Ended up at GABAN. Do you know them? They're one of the big six, based over on Lansbury Five – the Gollancz Arms, Books and Narcotics publishing conglomerate. At first everything was fine. The books were doing well, Cliff was really feeling like he'd hit a groove with the bee metaphors; it was all roses and extra sugar-lumps for me. But then his editor turned up one day, wanting an "important chat". Cliff had assumed it was going to be about his latest novel, but instead, they start telling him about this new wonder drug they'd got planned, some kind of energy pill. They were going to call it "Knuckle Down". Good, catchy name. And they wanted Cliff to be the face of it in their upcoming advertising campaign. There was a lot of talk about "synergy" and "cross market ferti-lisation". Of course, Cliff was delighted. Money for old rope so far as he was concerned. Didn't even have to get out of bed. But then, a couple of weeks later, he started hearing … rumours.'

'What kind of rumours?'

'They'd been doing this big drugs trial out on Proxima Twelve. And the word on the publishing grapevine was that things hadn't gone well. There'd been deaths. Lots of deaths. Look, Cliff wasn't a saint, and he'd put his name to some pretty shoddy quality merchandise – there's a Ganymede lunchbox that will take your fingers right off – but he had a *few* scruples. He wasn't going to endorse anything really dodgy. So he dug about for a bit, got a couple of old publishing contacts to ask around, and he managed to get hold of something. Here, I'll show you.'

The horse slid out of the chair and clip clopped over to a computer terminal set into the wall. He mashed the display with his nose for a bit, cursed under his breath, and eventually a file popped up. Phoebe, Glen and Misha crowded around to look at it. They read the title: *PRELIMINARY DATA ON THE ARBITRATAZINE ('KNUCKLE DOWN') TRIAL.*

'It's a confidential in-house report, not for general consumption. You're welcome to take it with you. There's

117

a lot of technical jargon in there about how they make the drug that I don't understand – I am, after all, just a horse – but, skip to page twenty, the section that's supposed to detail the side effects. There – look!'

Phoebe frowned. 'It's empty.'

'Exactly,' said the horse. 'No side effects listed at all! Well, Cliff's not an idiot. As soon as he saw that, it was pretty obvious what had happened. They'd *redacted* it! There was a cover-up afoot. So, he did some more digging, and then he found *this*.'

The horse bumped and licked the display until a graph popped up.

'That's the suicide rate on Proxima Twelve, and *that's* the six months when they were running the drugs trial.'

'Good grief,' said Phoebe. 'It goes through the roof.'

'Oh, yes,' said Misha. 'I remember now. That was big news back on Gippsworld. We've had the highest per capita suicide rate of all the planets in the system for as long as anyone can remember – it's one of the statistics we're most proud of – so this year, when Proxima Twelve knocked us off the top of the table, it was a real blow.'

The horse nodded. 'It's not *proof*, of course. There's no paper trail between the suicide spike and Knuckle Down. But Cliff took one look at that graph and decided he wanted out of the contract. Except it turned out old Marty Zeevon had done a pretty terrible deal back when he negotiated it. GABAN owned image, personality, appearance and opinion rights in perpetuity. Cliff retained T-shirt rights. Marty was always weirdly hot on T-shirt rights, you've got to give him that. Anyway, I'm afraid that's as much as I know. Cliff disappeared on the book tour, but I never received any more memories. Like I said, very strange.'

'You think that could be what's inside our mysterious

box?' said Glen, rubbing his chin in an unintentional pantomime of a Person Having A Rare Important Thought.
'The paper trail? The dirty on this drug?'

'Makes sense,' said Misha. 'You can see why they'd want
to keep it quiet.'

'Well, thanks horse,' said Phoebe. 'You've been extremely
helpful.'

'So what do we do now?' said Misha. Glen poured
himself another drink.

'I vote to stay here and pet the horse, drink the wine
cellar dry.'

'I'd certainly welcome the company,' said the horse. 'Tell
me – do you think Cliff is coming back any time soon?'

Phoebe and Misha both looked a bit uncomfortable.

'I'm afraid not, horse,' said Phoebe, after a difficult pause.

'Oh. I *see*,' said the horse, sadly. 'Was it peaceful?'

'Not very peaceful, no. Actually, we think he was
murdered. But don't worry – I'm a trained police officer
and I'm going to get to the bottom of this. And from what
you've said it looks like we need to pay a visit to his publisher.'

'But Cliff was a cash cow,' said Glen. 'A publisher
wouldn't murder a cash cow if they could help it, would
they?'

The horse pondered that for a moment and sighed. 'I
think the young lady might be right. To be honest, "being
alive" isn't very high up on the list of desirable traits an
author can have. These days it's more of a nuisance than
anything. I mean, look at Robert Ludlum. The man has
been dead for a millennium, but that hasn't seemed to get
in the way of him knocking out a new book every year.'

Chapter Twelve

'So you're the new interns?' said the receptionist.

'Yes, we are,' said Glen, doing his grinning trick again. 'The three of us are very keen to break into the cosmopolitan and rewarding world of publishing.'

They were standing in the cheerless glass and steel lobby of the GABAN Conglomerate's headquarters, a building that, according to the plaques on the door, had won *Architectural Exercises In Narcissism*'s Best Monolithic Embodiment of Dystopian Ennui Award six years running. Busy-looking people hurried back and forth. Lansbury Five's fluffy cyan clouds drifted past the windows in an unnecessarily smug way. Misha gazed up at a wall plastered with pictures of books he recognised from the bestseller lists. Next to those were pictures of popular drugs he recognised from the chemists. And next to those were a whole load of famous cluster bombs and landmines he recognised from various blood-drenched news reports.

'You'll need to sign here.' The receptionist hit a button and beamed a pop-up to their retina displays. 'It's a simple waiver saying that we're not responsible for any workplace deaths, including but not limited to your getting mashed up by giant cogs, toxic fume inhalation, and basic exhaustion. Here are your badges. Orientation is up on level two. I hope you have a long and prolific career!'

The trio followed the signs marked 'Orientation Seminar' and took their seats at the back of an over-lit conference room stuffed full of other, actual, bright-eyed young interns. A looping holographic recording played in the air above them. The familiar fist-shaped GABAN Conglomerate logo spun across the room and then dissolved into the image of a young woman, pretty and emaciated, as she approached a young man, slightly less emaciated, by a water cooler.

'Hi! First day at Gollancz?' said the man.

'It is, yes! I'm raring to go! My name's Marcy!' said the woman.

'Nice to meet you, Marcy! I'm Mike! You're going to love it here. Perhaps you'd like to hear a little bit about the company?'

'That would be super!'

'Well, GABAN Corp was one of the survivors of the Lansbury System's media conflagration from all the way back in the 25th century. We started off as a boutique publishing imprint, specialising in romance fiction, but over the years we've branched out into arms dealing, fashion, and legal narcotics.'

'That sounds like quite a departure, Mike!'

'Not really, Marcy. You see, whether you're trying to sell a novel, a lipstick, a K-30 Assault Rifle, or a new type of sobriety pill, ultimately, it all comes down to two things – good marketing and a flexible moral outlook. And those are qualities we in the book trade already had in spades.'

'So let me get one thing straight – as an intern, am I technically a slave?'

'I'm afraid not, Marcy! As you know, slavery IS legal in this system, but there's a lot of annoying red tape involved, and slaves have many rights for the duration of their service that just aren't practical in a forward-facing business like publishing. Don't worry, though! Things might seem tough at first, but work hard and there's a swift career progression. I used to be a regular intern just like you, but now, after a mere sixteen years, I'm a level two intern, so in addition to travel expenses I receive a weekly allocation of nutrient paste deemed sufficient to sustain virtually all necessary life functions.'

Marcy turned to the camera, and gave it a cheery grin.

*'Great! That's something to aspire to! No more working bleak
nights near the underpass for me!'*

'Do you have any other questions, Marcy?'

'What's the health plan like, Mike?'

*'It's very comprehensive. The basic gist is that if you die, you'll
agree to let us use your organs, bones and general viscera for the
production of glue, paper and other essential office supplies. Because
we care about the environment, the GABAN promise is that none of
our intern's spent carcasses go to waste.'*

Marcy and Mike gabbed on chirpily for a little while,
then the display flicked off again and an elderly man with
a stoop stood up at the front of the room and coughed.
'Under your seats you'll find a slip. The colour of that slip
indicates which department you've been assigned to,' he
said, in a bored monotone. 'Report to the relevant duty
manager, and welcome to your new lives of being able to
tell people at parties that you've got a job in the media.'

He sat back down again. Phoebe looked at her slip, which
was green. 'I'm in Design. How about you two?'

'Correspondence,' said Misha.

'Innovation strategy,' said Glen.

'Okay, we'll meet back at the canteen at lunch. Try to
find out whatever you can. But be *subtle* about it.' Phoebe
shot Glen a pointed look. 'We don't want to make people
suspicious.'

Phoebe followed the rest of the green slip interns down
to a vast basement lined with row upon row of input termi-
nals. A thousand sets of eyes momentarily flicked up from
a sea of wan faces illuminated only by the glow of their
screens, and then instantly flicked back down again. An
officious senior intern with a greyish sheen to his skin sat
Phoebe down at a desk and pointed at her terminal. 'Intern

Clag,' he said, checking his notes. 'You've been assigned to poignant shoe duty.'

'Great,' said Phoebe. 'What's poignant shoe duty?'

'It's what it sounds like. You locate copyright-free images of children's empty shoes. You then tint those images sepia. We're a big publisher, and that means we require a minimum of five hundred new sepia images of poignant empty shoes for our fiction and memoir covers every day. If you fail to meet that target you will be docked an hour's rest period. Bear in mind that as a level one intern you have a forty minute total rest allocation for the week. Stimulants may be taken, but please note that only GABAN branded narcotics are allowed on site.'

* * *

Nine hours later Phoebe slumped onto an uncomfortable canteen bench and put her head on the table. She groaned. When she managed to sit up again, she saw that Misha was there, covered in cuts and soot. Glen was there too, and he, inevitably, looked fine.

'So many shoes,' said Phoebe. 'I can't feel my fingers.'

'This place is terrible,' said Misha, nodding miserably.

'What have they got you doing?'

'I'm on the slush pile.'

'Reading manuscripts? That doesn't sound so bad.'

'We don't *read* them,' said Misha with a hollow-sounding laugh. 'There's sixteen billion sent in from across the galaxy every minute. They all get instantly wiped from the mail system. But to delete that amount of data means the server runs incredibly hot. It's my job to help keep the cooling pipes unclogged. There's a lot of shovelling heavy blocks of ice, but we still had six fires before midday.'

'How about you, Glen?'

'Mine isn't too bad,' said Glen, with a relaxed shrug. 'Up in innovation strategy we just have to make up new names for products that haven't worked out for some reason or another. Like, we had this prototype that was meant to be a 'My First Chemical Peel' sort of thing. You know, for kids, right? But it kept on melting the test subject's faces. So they flipped it over to the arms division, and we got tasked with coming up with an exciting-sounding name for it. I got highly commended for "Mallowiser4000", because it kind of leaves you looking like a marshmallow. Similar texture, too. They're trying to choose between that and "Face Repurposer".'

'I don't suppose either of you actually *found out* anything?' said Phoebe.

'I didn't have a chance,' said Misha.

'I clean forgot,' said Glen.

Phoebe sighed. 'I didn't have much luck, either. I talked to a couple of people, in the few seconds when the senior intern had his back turned, but nobody has even *met* anyone from editorial. They're on the 17th floor apparently, and nobody ever gets to go up there. The place is riddled with security drones.'

A klaxon sounded to indicate the end of their three-minute lunch break.

'Okay,' said Phoebe. 'Let's try again. See you in nine hours.'

Phoebe rejoined the shuffling queue of interns heading back down towards the design gulag. Feeling slightly light-headed, she found herself drifting into the middle of a daydream in which Sergeant Peterson was pinning a medal to her shirt. *You've done a fantastic job cracking the Ganymede case wide open,*' he was saying. *'And to mark this glorious day for our little police force we will be stuffing your colleague Alicia into a cannon and firing her at the nearest sun. That's not excessive – that's the least you deserve, Officer Clag.'* Peterson smiled, and then he morphed into a stream of dancing noodle pots.

A little way ahead of her a commotion and a strangulated cry brought her back to the moment. One of the interns, a skinny, curly-haired youth who had a face the colour of dead jellyfish, had collapsed to the floor. 'I can't do it,' the intern wailed. 'I can't look at *one* more picture of an empty swing or a pensive woman's back.' Other interns tried to drag him to his feet, but he went on sobbing. The constantly hovering security drones all surged towards him. Phoebe suddenly realised that, for the next few seconds at least, nobody was watching her. She tiptoed across the corridor and ducked into a stairwell. Behind her she heard a zapping sound and a scream and a request for the cleaner to mop up a spillage.

* * *

Seventeen flights of stairs later Phoebe paused, dry-heaved a bit, contemplated the wisdom of what her diet was doing for her in terms of cardio-vascular fitness, and then slipped through a door and onto the editorial floor. Another flinty-looking receptionist blocked her way.

'Hi there,' said Phoebe, thinking on her feet and waving her green slip. 'I'm from design.' She rummaged in her pocket and held up an old noodle wrapper. 'Got a couple of covers to run past the editor of the Cliff Ganymede *In Memoriam* anthology.'

The receptionist pursed his lips. 'There's no appointment in the book. And editors don't usually get bothered with that kind of thing.'

'I know – it's just there's been a hiccup. Hard to believe, but we've completely run out of images of poignant empty shoes.'

'Good grief,' said the receptionist, looking alarmed.

'Exactly. So we were thinking of going with either a sad bee or the silhouette of a sad bee. My boss is keen to move this along, and you'd be doing me a real favour; we've got a backlog as long as your arm – that time of year, I guess – and so I *hoped*—'

'Fine, fine,' said the receptionist, cutting her off and waving her down the hallway. 'He's at lunch at the moment, but you can leave it on his desk.'

Phoebe found the office with a pile of old Cliff Ganymede books stacked up under a glass coffee table, and darted inside. She was so pleased to have got this far that it was only now, when confronted with working out her next move, that she found herself yet again at a bit of a loss.

'Come on, Clag,' she said out loud to herself. 'This is your big chance to prove your detectiving skills. Find some evidence. Something incriminating.'

She glanced around for anything that looked incriminating, and instantly realised that she didn't really know what incriminating things looked like. She sat down at the editor's desk, and tapped the built-in display, but, predictably, it asked for a password. From what Phoebe could remember of those pulpy detective shows, a clue to the password was usually *hidden in plain sight*. All she could see was a half-eaten banana. She shrugged and decided to eat the rest of it. Then she typed 'BANANA'. Nothing happened.

'Why is this all so much more *difficult* than on TV?' she muttered.

'Excuse me.'

Phoebe swallowed hard, looked up and saw a man with a nice suit and a slick haircut leaning against the doorframe.

'Ah,' said Phoebe, wondering if she had any chance of reaching the elevators before the security drones vaporised her. 'I realise this probably seems bad, but it's not what it looks like.'

'I know who you are,' said the man, laughing.

'You do?'

'Don't worry, I'm not calling security. Not yet, anyway,' he closed the door behind him and walked over to a drinks cabinet. 'This happens from time to time. Truth is, I admire your moxy.' The man poured out a tumbler of gin and looked at his watch. 'Okay, you've got ten seconds to impress me, let's hear it.'

'Hear what?'

'Your *pitch*. I assume, from the condition of your hair and the stains on your shirt, that you're an aspiring author, right? Sneaking in here to wow me with your precious idea that you are convinced is unique as a snowflake. So, what is it?'

Phoebe thought for a moment. 'It's about a murder,' she said.

'A kid?'

'Not a kid, no.'

'Make it a kid. Murdered kids are always a draw. People can't get enough of murdered kids.'

'Fair enough. Anyway, there's this girl trying to solve the case …'

'What's the girl's job?'

'Police woman?'

'Can we make her an archaeologist?'

'Sure.'

'But she's got issues, right? Something relatable like OCD, or mild Asperger's?'

'She has some body image issues.'

'That's good. And has she got a hot beefcake secretary?'

'Do archaeologists have secretaries?'

'You tell me, kid, you're the author,' the editor frowned. 'Five more seconds before I throw you out, by the way.'

'Okay, yes, she has a hot secretary and, uh, she discovers a plot involving a terrible new narcotic that has awful side effects.'

'Eh,' the editor pulled a face. 'Drug fiction isn't that exciting in the current market-place. You know what sells? Thargoids. Look, you're the writer – it's not my place to suggest things, but let me just throw this out there: she's got body image issues, but she's *also* got OCD. And there's this Thargoid gang, who have OCD themselves, and they're killing the kids in alphabetical order. Only our heroine can spot the pattern, because – I don't know – something archaeological. How about that?'

'It doesn't make a *lot* of sense,' said Phoebe.

'Okay, well, you had your shot,' said the editor, sounding a bit petulant. 'I think I'm calling security now.'

He leaned forward to activate the intercom. Desperate, Phoebe decided to try a different, more direct tack.

'I'm not an author. I'm with the police,' she flashed her badge and hoped he didn't have a chance to read the details too closely. 'And before you call security, there's something you should know. *We have the Lenslok box.*' She paused, letting the significance of that sink in.

'Do you?' said the editor.

'It's in a very safe place, before you get any ideas.'

'That's good. I guess that it must be a really nice box, then? Do you have some special emotional attachment to it?'

Phoebe faltered for a moment. This wasn't how this sort of conversation played out in the detective books.

'I think you know what's inside it,' she said.

'I do?'

'Yes. And we know too,' she lied.

They eyeballed each other wordlessly.

'Anyhoo,' the editor looked at his watch again after the eyeballing had reached the minute mark, 'how long is this staring thing likely to take, by the way? I've got a two o'clock with Agatha Tate.'

'The crime writer? Oh, is she doing another Inspector Moon-Squid? I love those,' said Phoebe, momentarily forgetting herself. She paused, then fixed him once more with a serious stare. 'Look. Do I have to say what's in the box?'

The editor held his hands up. 'If you must.'

Fine, thought Phoebe, *he's trying to bluff it. Two can play at that game.* 'The box contains proof – hard irrefutable proof – that your experimental energy-boosting drug, known as "Knuckle Down", has a horrific, fatal side effect. It makes people top themselves.'

'Ah,' said the editor. 'Is that so?'

'It is,' said Phoebe.

The editor stood up, closed the blinds, and then came back to the desk. He waved a hand at the holo-display.

'Jenkins, can you bring in the Knuckle Down File. The one we have for the Cliff Ganymede cross-promotion?'

An intern came in clutching a secure document ball. The editor flicked it on, and passed it over to Phoebe.

'I'm under no obligation to share this with you. I've seen from your badge that you're about five parsecs outside of your customs and excise jurisdiction, but we at Gollancz are an open, honest company with nothing to hide. Here, read it. Take your time.'

Phoebe looked at the file being projected by the ball into her lap. She read it for a few minutes. Then she read it again. The editor whistled to himself, and waited politely for her to finish.

129

'Well …' Phoebe stammered after a while. 'It's a fake. Same as the one Ganymede had. Obviously you've done a fake report.'

'Look at the cover. It's not even *our* report, Ms Clag, it's the results of the GDA's exhaustive and independently monitored tests.'

Phoebe stared at the Galactic Drug Administration's seal. It seemed legit.

'I'm not saying we've never released a drug that didn't have an unpleasant pharmacological side effect,' the editor continued. 'I mean, good lord, we publish a sun-cream that's left a dozen people pregnant. Our health and safety measures are not very rigorous at all. But Knuckle Down isn't like that. It is one of the few drugs we've produced that has, in fact, zero chemical side effects.'

'But Ganymede … he had the leaked report. And I've seen the graph. The suicide spike. The subjects all killed themselves.'

'Yes, that's true.'

Phoebe started to get the same feeling she got when talking to Glen.

'Knuckle Down has zero *chemical* side effects. But that isn't to say it's flawless. It does, in fact, have one massive flaw.'

He paused, and gave her a slightly sad, sombre smile. 'It works.'

Phoebe looked at him, confused. 'It works? That's the flaw?'

'It's not some common or garden *stimulant*. It's not an energy booster. It's a whole other kettle of fish.' The editor downed his drink. He leaned forward and lowered his voice. 'The test subjects who took Knuckle Down stopped dithering. They stopped procrastinating. Instead of writing out lists of all the things they intended to do one day, they just did those things. Instead of drawing up fancy schedules for their revision, they revised. Instead of saying that from *tomorrow* morning I'm going to start running five miles a day, they just ran five miles. Straight away! No option, because the drug makes your hypothalamus itch like crazy if you procrastinate. See, human brains are actually pretty great at knowing what they should be doing, they're just useless at acting on that knowledge for any timescale longer than about five minutes. But subjects on Knuckle Down focused and they worked hard. The results were –' he actually shuddered at this point – 'horrific.' The editor opened a drawer in the desk, pulled out a packet of GABAN branded cigarettes and lit one. 'The guy who'd always wanted to write his novel, but who had never been able to sit down and do it, did it. And when he'd done it, that novel turned out to be terrible. Poorly characterised nonsense. Or, worse, it turned out to be *pretty good*, but he didn't know anybody who knew anybody in order to get an agent. The girl who'd wanted to take the legal exams so she could progress in her company took the exams, aced them even, but then it turned out that her company was run by dolts, and so she still didn't get promoted. Or sometimes somebody *would* get the promotion, but it turned out the new job was just as point-less and unfulfilling as the old one, and the extra money didn't make the girl in accounts fancy the guy in human resources like he thought it might. Neither did successfully losing a few pounds off some chunky thighs. You see, we've done a lot of research. We've combed through untold reams of data. And "hard work" isn't the key to anything. The idiots and the affluent triumph regardless. I mean, maybe if we could develop a drug to turn people into egregious, grasping bastards, we'd be onto something. Believe me, we've probably got teams of R and D guys working on it.'

He took a long drag on the cigarette and then flicked it into a bin. 'Knuckle Down is a drug that exposes a difficult truth. It turns out our collective sanity is preserved by a single, fragile concept – the idea that one day, if we could just get down to it, if we could just stop watching TV *for ten fucking minutes*, we could change everything for the better. Pull that rug out from under civilisation's feet and everything goes to hell. Once someone knows that actually, this time, they really *did* try their best, and yet their lives are *still* a cosmic joke, they tend to lose perspective. Or gain perspective, I suppose you could argue. Whatever – the result is the same: they usually jump in front of the nearest hyperloop shuttle.'

'So why are you releasing it?' said Phoebe, boggling at him. 'If you know it's going to cause untold misery, why don't you *do* something?'

'What am *I* supposed to do?'

'You could stop it! You're in charge!'

'Me?' the editor laughed. 'I'm an intern.'

'But you're the editor-in-chief.'

'Yes, and I've been here forty years now, but nobody on the editorial side is *paid* anymore. It's interns all the way up. Best not let on to everyone downstairs; they might find it demotivating. Knuckle Down is going ahead because Marketing says it's going ahead. They've got the galaxywide roll-out planned. They're the ones that call the shots. And they've run it past our guys in legal a hundred times. Legal says it's fine. Gollancz will be completely blameless for any resulting suicidal activity. The culprit is the galaxy. The stupid, capricious, non-meritocratic galaxy.'

Phoebe looked despairingly at the floor. 'Did you murder Cliff Ganymede?' she asked quietly.

'If you're going to get your knickers in a twist each time a publisher happens to kill an author, we'll be here all day.

Not that I'm admitting anything. But Ganymede was going to cause us a PR headache. He was the kind of person people listened to. So my guess is Marketing … took steps. How they went about that is their own business. I'm not really minded to say anything more about the matter.'

The editor walked around the desk to Phoebe, and put his hand on her shoulder. 'Look, Officer Clag, my advice – leave well alone. The marketing people. Their *eyes*. Like looking into holes Satan pissed into a glacier. You don't mess with them.' He paused, then frowned. 'By the way, did you see half a banana in here? I haven't eaten for six days. I'll swap you a corporate stress ball for any spare nutrient paste you happen to have. God, interning can be tough.'

* * *

'… so that's that,' said Phoebe, as, back at the canteen, she gloomily finished recounting her run in with the editor. 'There's nothing we can do. Alicia was right. I haven't got a clue about real police work. We've got exactly *nowhere*. We still don't even know what's in that dumb box, but whatever it is, it's obviously not a top secret drugs report. I'm stumped.' She tore off her intern badge and threw it at one of the buzzing security drones. 'Let's get back to the *Lili Damita* and go home, I've had it with this place.'

'We can't just give up,' said Misha, anxious that the end of their investigation meant the end of his being able to hang out with her.

'Phoebe's right. It seems to me we've given it our best shot,' said Glen, throwing his badge away too. 'But there comes a point where you've just got to put your hands up and say – this will remain a mystery, same as magnets and wind and fish and all the other unexplainable wonders of the universe. No reason to beat ourselves up over it. And besides, you know what this means, dollface?'

Phoebe shook her head.

'It means it's time to fulfil your end of our bargain.' He stood up, fished in his pocket for his keys and clicked the little fob that would get the *Lili Damita* warmed up ready for them. 'Come on, I'm taking you to dinner.'

'Glen, I'm not really in the mood.'

'You promised. And a deal's a deal. Besides, I know a really good place just down the coast from here. Best novelty fine-dining on the whole of Lansbury Five. Maurice, you'll be okay to entertain yourself for the evening?' He winked at Misha. 'Don't wait up or anything.'

* * *

Misha paced up and down the ship's cabin, stared out of the window at the bleak concrete sprawl of the restaurant's parking lot, and tried not to think about how the dinner date might be going.

He sat down on one of the couches and called up a title from the online Ganymede library. Then he digitally paid an extra credit and switched the Interactive Bonus Feature on. Cliff's avuncular face appeared on the flight console's holographic display.

'Hello BULGAKOV, MISHA,' said the Interactive Bonus Feature. 'You've purchased one THREE MINUTE personalised advice session. What's bothering you, son?'

'Cliff,' said Misha. 'I'm having trouble. There's a girl I like, but I don't seem to be getting anywhere with her.'

'I'm sorry to hear this BULGAKOV, MISHA,' said the Interactive Bonus Feature. 'Did you try to drop vibrant-sounding words into your conversation to emphasise your sexual potency?'

134

'Yes, I already did that. And I told her about my unique snoring. All that stuff.'

The hologram nodded and did a knowledgeable frown. 'Well BULGAKOV, MISHA, men and women are like bees. When bees seek a mating partner they'll attempt to put on a courtship display. The bees will line up in the hive and each bee has thirty seconds – approximately a week in bee years – to really grab the attention of a panel of bee judges. The showiest bee will then get to mate with the Emperor or Empress Bee.'

'So I should do some sort of waggle dance?'

'Not a literal waggle dance. But something like a waggle dance. Something bold.'

'Oh well, thanks Cliff. The trouble is,' said Misha, switching the book off again with a doleful wave of his hand, 'that doesn't really sound like me at all.'

* * *

'Pretty swish, right?' said Glen, refilling Phoebe's glass.

Phoebe looked around at the restaurant Glen had taken her to and grudgingly admitted to herself that it was, indeed, pretty swish. She picked up her knife, sliced another chunk off their table, and popped it into her mouth.

'It's certainly high concept,' she said. 'Carving out a restaurant from the inside of the biggest naturally occurring truffle ever found. The smell is slightly overpowering, though.'

'Seriously, eat as much of the table as you want,' said Glen, helping himself to a chunk of the wall. 'My dad's got an expense account here.'

'You have a ridiculous lifestyle, Glen.'

'Thank you,' said Glen, with a serious nod. 'But that's not enough. I'm not content. The truth is, Pheebs, my days are a terrible, endless parade of meaningless encounters with svelte, model-quality women. But you're different, you're not like them.'

'Thanks,' said Phoebe. 'I suppose.'

'Also, and I don't want you to take this the wrong way, but I think it's important to face facts. You're not getting any younger. And your cybernetic leg is strange and off-putting to most people, though luckily I find it to be kind of a turn-on. That's not a kink you can rely on finding in other guys,' Glen leaned forward. 'Look, I know you think I'm not a serious person, but that's not the case. Sure, maybe you were right, maybe this pirate thing *was* a fad. But my next project isn't a fad. And I want you to be a part of it.'

'A part of what?'

Glen indicated the restaurant around them with an expansive sweep of his arm. 'I'm seriously considering getting into the restaurant business.'

'You're buying this place?'

'Not *this* – I think the giant fungus dining experience is close to being played out. But I've got some amazing ideas for an entire new chain. Do you want to hear about my concept?' Glen waved her closer and lowered his voice to a whisper. 'People send in pictures of their deceased loved ones when they make a booking. And I get all the waiters to undergo instamatic surgery to look *just like those dead relatives*. So you'll get your main course served by your dear old grandma, and your pudding by your dead fiancé or something.'

'Wow,' said Phoebe, actually impressed that Glen always seemed able to find some genuine new way to surprise her.

'It gets better. The restaurant will *revolve*. And the entire menu will be themed around synthetic noodles. You love synthetic noodles.'

Phoebe nodded. 'I do.'

'Which is why I want you to manage it. We'd be a team.'

'WHY DON'T WE HAVE A *VENUSIAN* HISTORY MONTH?' said the hen, nodding at the waiter.

Phoebe idly wondered why Glen had brought his annoying pet to a romantic meal. The hen grinned at her.

'I've just noticed,' said Phoebe. 'Does your hen have teeth?'

'Of course it does, beak dental-augmentation, I'm not a luddite.' Glen took one of her hands in his. 'So come on, what do you say?'

'Look, Glen. I'm not saying none of it was fun when we were dating, in a mind-bendingly stupid kind of way ...'

'It was! It *was* fun. We're *good* together. You and me, we're like the ingredients to a pie. You're like the baking soda – useless on your own – and like I'm another ingredient, a slightly better ingredient than baking soda, eggs maybe. Or celery.'

'Celery?'

'The point is, you put those ingredients together and they suddenly work.'

'I don't know. Baking soda and celery? It sounds like a pretty disgusting pie, Glen.'

'It's a metaphor, babe.'

Phoebe suddenly stared at him.

'What? What is it? Have I got food on my face?' Glen dabbed at himself with a napkin.

'Ingredients!' exclaimed Phoebe.

Glen smiled at her as if she were an endearingly slow child. 'Yes, cupcake, that's what I'm trying to tell you. We're like ingredients.'

'No. The *ingredients*.' Phoebe pushed her truffle chair back and stood up. 'We need to get back to the ship.'

'What about us?' said Glen, looking exasperated. 'Are we an item again?'

'What? Oh, sure, whatever.'

She downed her glass of wine, and ran out of the restaurant. Glen shook his head and clicked his fingers at the waiter. 'Jesus. Chicks, man.'

'WHY ARE WOMEN SO SELF-ENTITLED?' said the hen.

'Shut up, hen,' said Glen.

* * *

'Misha!' shouted Phoebe, as she barrelled in through the door of the *Lili Damita*.

'What?' said Misha, frantically stabbing at the remote. 'It just turned to that channel automatically.'

'Ingredients!' Phoebe ran across to the flight console, not listening to him. 'We've been so busy looking at the *effects* of the drug, we forgot to look at the *ingredients*.'

Misha stared at her blankly.

'What if the mysterious box wasn't the reason they put a hit on you?'

'Well, of course it was the box,' said Misha. 'What other reason could there be?'

Phoebe called up a copy of Cliff's confidential drug report and the digital wallpaper was replaced by a dense pile of text. She flicked through a few pages. Then she stopped, and zoomed in on something. 'Look. Look there.'

Misha looked. 'What about it?'

'Read the *words*.'

Misha read the paragraph she was pointing to:

'Artificial synthesis of the main active ingredient, [henceforth to be referred to as compound X] has proven to be a dead end. The only naturally occurring source of the chemical is the Apostasioidae scrufus plant. Unfortunately cultivation of these plants is not possible on any planet other than the world to which they are native (see Appendix 6 for speculation as to why this may be so). Because this is a naturally

occurring compound we will not be able to copyright it. Therefore it is vital, prior to public announcement of Knuckle Down, to secure a monopoly on the supplies of Apostasioidae scrufus plants.

Misha shrugged. 'I'm still not following.'

'Come on, Misha, keep up. The *pigs*. That's what they were interested in. Not the stupid box, the pigs. That hit was targeting *you*. It just happened, by coincidence, to be the same day you'd picked to try your hand at intergalactic smuggling. Some poor sap must be wondering where his antique vase is.'

'So you mean, the publishers ...'

'... *want your pig farm*. They want a pig monopoly. They were trying to drive you out of business by blowing up your transport barn. Force your dad to sell up.'

Misha blanched. He flipped on a comms channel, and dialled the number home. It went to voicemail. 'He's not answering. Oh, Laika's biscuits! We need to get back to Gippsworld *right now*.'

The *Lili Damita*'s door hissed open again, and Glen and his hen sauntered up the ramp.

'Did she tell you the news?' said Glen.

'Yes!' said Misha. 'It was the pigs all along!'

'No, I meant about us being an item again.'

Glen grinned. Misha felt all the blood drain from his face and pool somewhere around his ankles. Phoebe did an awkward little shrug and examined her fingernails.

'I've got poor posture and a monstrous leg,' she mumbled, defensively. 'And I really like noodles.'

Misha swallowed very hard. 'Congratulations,' he said.

'You've turned a weird sort of colour,' said Glen. 'Are you feeling okay?'

'Probably space-flu,' said Misha.

139

Chapter Thirteen

They didn't have to wait for a landing slot, because the *Lili Damita* was the only ship in the entire New Vladimir Putingrad spaceport. All the traders' fancy out-of-town Pythons and Panthers and Asps had vanished. The Samaritans banner was back up in the arrivals lounge and dirt had started to gunge up the windows of the air traffic control tower again. As they exited through a deserted duty free shop the familiar acid sting of the planet's atmosphere hit Misha at the back of his throat like an old friend. Phoebe and Glen both made the sort of faces people tended to make when first stepping onto Gippsworld.

'This is worse than Bloomsbury Alpha,' said Glen, wrapping a scarf over his mouth, then pulling on a hair net for good measure. 'And Bloomsbury Alpha is one big sewage processing plant.'

'We bid for the same contract,' said Misha, sounding slightly wistful. 'The Bloomsburians have never let us forget it. Unfortunately, the sewage company felt Gippsworld didn't have the requisite level of élan to reflect their effluent-based brand.'

'Why is it all so *quiet*?' said Phoebe, surveying the boarded-up artisanal bakery and the empty array of galleries. 'This doesn't seem much like a planet in the middle of an unexpected art boom.'

Misha frowned, because she had a point. He stuck out a thumb and flagged down a solitary passing hover taxi.

They piled into the back. To Misha's surprise, he saw that it was Vitali behind the wheel.

'Vitali!'

'Oh, hey, Misha,' said Vitali, with a sleepy smile. 'Where to?'

'The farm, thanks. And if you could put your foot down, that would be great.' Misha looked at where Vitali's conical hat and kaftan now lay crumpled in the glove compartment. 'What happened? Where are all the traders? And why are you driving a taxi? I thought you were a leading light of the Outsider Art Movement now?'

'Oh, man, where have you been?' Vitali let out a rueful little laugh. 'It all went wrong. It all went wrong.'

'What do you mean?'

'You really don't *know*?'

Misha shook his head. Vitali rolled his eyes and started to explain. 'Happened a few days ago. I turned up at the mineshaft as usual with some new pieces – my best work to date, I'd really started to get the hang of making faces look more like faces – but nobody was around. There were no traders at all. So I took a trip up to the *Jim Bergerac*, and same deal: nobody was interested. Poor Yevgeny was distraught, going on about how much he'd spent to have the *Omar Sharif*'s carpets shampooed, wanting to know where everyone had disappeared to. Still, I figured it was just an off day. But, next morning – exact same thing! I slashed the prices on *A Remembrance of Cows* and *Unhappy Residue*. Didn't do any good. Suddenly, couldn't even *give* the things away. And it wasn't only me, it was like that for everyone.'

'That's terrible,' said Misha, half meaning it. 'But how come you're not just kicking back? You must have already made a fortune, right? You guys were raking it in.'

141

'Yeah, not so much. I blew through a fair chunk of it. A lot of us did. There was a sudden craze for cosmetic surgery, you know, the stuff that makes you look like zoo animals, like on the TV show.' Vitali leaned forward and pointed to where a small tail was now poking through the back of his trousers. 'And good surgeons don't come cheap. Seems a bit silly in retrospect. One of those collective hysteria things, I guess. The real problem is that we had another city meeting a little while back, and the President thought it would be a good idea for us all to invest in something called the Gippsworld Outsider Art Fund. Showed us a lot of nice graphs. Well, you can probably guess what happened: that crashed pretty badly the same morning all the traders disappeared. Turns out "investing in yourself" isn't such a hot idea. Not when yourselves are us, at any rate.'

Vitali sighed, and the taxi came to a juddering halt. 'Anyway, here we are. That'll be two credits. Though I also accept payment in leftover food or cardboard to help build the rest of my shelter. My habitation pod got repossessed.'

Misha handed Vitali his last couple of credits, commiserated again about how things had gone, and sprinted up the path to the farmhouse. To his relief, he found Misha Senior sitting out on the porch flipping through a gossip magazine, apparently unharmed.

'Dad! You're okay!' Misha bounded across the porch and hugged him. 'I've left about a dozen messages!'

Misha Senior extricated himself awkwardly from the hug.

'Of course I am okay. Why you do vulgar public display of affection? This is the womanish behaviour of a methane farmer.'

'I thought they might have done something terrible to you.'

Misha paused, and looked his father up and down. He frowned.

'Why are you wearing a suit?'

His father scratched his neck and looked away. 'I like suit. Why should I not wear suit? Who died and made you king fashion man?'

Misha narrowed his eyes. 'You only wear that suit for special occasions. Aunt Lushka's funeral. The year we beat Lansbury Five in the atmo-surfing bowl. The time our prize-pig won best-in-show. Why is *today* a special occasion?'

'I do not know what you talk about,' muttered Misha Senior evasively.

'And why weren't you answering my calls?'

'You ask all these questions. What about *my* questions? Where is transport barn? Why you disappear for entire week? Who is this girl? Why her posture so poor? Who is this man? Why his teeth so shiny?'

Glen and Phoebe, loitering self-consciously behind Misha, waved.

'I asked first, dad – why weren't you answering my calls?'

'I was out.'

'Where?'

'I was having dinner.'

Misha fixed him with a hard stare. Misha Senior pouted. 'Fine. If you must know: I was having dinner with top movie star Zargella Lombard.'

'Oh no.'

'She turns out to be very stupid woman. I tell her many pig farming anecdotes. I tell her the funny story about our threshing machine accidents. I tell her about smells to be

143

found in pig silo. I tell her about time I have the foot-rot. She does not laugh once at these stories, even though they are all A1 good anecdotes. She spends whole dinner picking at food like bird. I ask if she does not like the goulash. I make it myself, using all the best Gippsworld parasites. She says she is watching what she eats. I compliment her sturdy thighs. After an hour she says, "Okey-dokey, that's my time done, I'm out of here." Then she leaves! I get no kiss.'

Misha's stomach lurched. 'How did you come to be having dinner with Zargella Lombard, dad?'

'Fine, you make me say it: I swap dinner date for pig farm,' said Misha Senior. He shrugged, and folded his arms.

'You can't have done,' said Misha, slapping his forehead.

'I'm afraid he has,' said a voice from behind them.

Misha turned round to see an urbane man with a phosphorescent cravat and a white Zirconium suit coming up the path towards the farmstead. It took Misha a moment to recognise him as the mysterious stranger who had gotten everyone so excited about Gippsworld indigenous art in the first place.

'And, now the paperwork has gone through, as of this morning you are both on private property owned by the Gollancz Arms, Books and Narcotics Publishing Conglomerate, of which I happen to be Senior Head of Marketing. I'm going to have to ask you to leave.'

The man doffed his hat, walked past them into the farmhouse with an airy saunter and slammed the door shut behind him in quite a pointed way. Misha Senior looked sheepishly at Misha. 'Why you so upset?' he said. 'You hate pig farming. You always badgering me to sell farm. You are fickle son.'

'Dad, how could you? For one dinner date!'

'Not only date,' said Misha Senior, brightening up a bit. 'Shares in Gippsworld art-fund.'

Misha groaned.

'It is not my fault. I am lonely. Zargella Lombard remind me of your mother. Similar stout neck and fleshy back before threshing machine accident. I an old man. Do not be angry with me.'

'This is touching,' said the Senior Head of Marketing, sticking his head back out of the door, and coughing politely. 'But I really *am* going to have to insist you get off the property. Listen, though, no hard feelings – take a card.'

He handed Misha a card. It said 'PUBLISHING INTERN OPPORTUNITIES, GIPPSWORLD PIG IMPRINT' next to a toll-free number.

'There's a coupon on the back that gives you 25% off your first order of Knuckle Down. Launches this winter. It's the get-up-and-go drug all your friends will be talking about.'

The door slammed shut again.

Misha looked beseechingly at Phoebe. 'Can't you do something?' he said.

'We've got no evidence of criminal wrong-doing, Misha,' Phoebe replied, giving him an apologetic shrug. 'I think it's over. I'm sorry.'

'In that case,' said Glen, 'is it too much to hope there's somewhere on this wretched planet that we can get a drink?'

* * *

'You know what my trouble is?' said the President, watching sadly as two men in Gollancz overalls took down from above the sandwich bar the painting of him wrestling the creatures. 'I tried to fly too high. I'm like Icarus. And Gippsworld is like the melted wax in my wings. But I swear to you, I was just trying to do the best for this place.'

145

'Icarus didn't try to fly for the benefit of the wax in his wings, did he?' said Phoebe, leaning on the counter of the Spaceport's Bar and Grill while a baristabot poured them all some unappetising milkshakes. They'd found the President sitting out in the street, tearing up election posters, and had dragged him inside before the constant driving rain gave him pneumonia.

'Well, no, the analogy doesn't entirely work. Maybe Gippsworld is Icarus and I'm the wax. I've lost track. Point is – I'm a terrible president.'

'Don't be so hard on yourself,' said Misha. 'You didn't know.'

'I didn't! I really didn't. I mean, *perhaps* I should have asked a few more questions. But he seemed so keen to help out. He said that with just a small investment from what was left of our municipal budget, he could transform our fortunes. And the next day, the very next day, we turned out to all be fantastically talented indigenous outsider artists!' The President paused. 'Like magic. In retrospect that did seem a little too good to be true.'

'Why are they taking down your pictures?' asked Misha.

'They're closing this place, turning it into a public relations office. I sold all the civically owned leases in order to invest in their Outsider Art Fund. You've got to spend money to make money, that's what he said. Again, seemed to make more sense at the time.'

There was a clang from outside, as a tank-sized demolition bot knocked the Gippsworld Spaceport sign off the control tower.

'And we're not going to be called Gippsworld anymore,' added the President. 'As of tomorrow we're Bio-Agri Product World 69-d. It's not as catchy. We'll need new headed notepaper. What a disaster.'

146

The President downed some more of his drink, and then started singing a miserable old Gippsworld folk song about a foot-rot epidemic.

'I'm really sorry it didn't work out better, Misha,' said Phoebe.

'Yeah, it sucks,' said Glen. 'It's a shame about your farming business, and it's a shame that untold millions are going to die because of this terrible drug. But let's not forget the *upside*: at least this whole sorry escapade finally brought me and Phoebe back together.'

'Yes,' said Misha, staring at the bottom of his glass. 'I suppose it did at least do that.'

'Anyhow, it's getting late,' said Glen, yawning. He put an arm round Phoebe. 'We should really be leaving these guys to it. How do you fancy maxing and relaxing in my time-share over on Kembel?'

Phoebe sighed. 'Why not? It's not like I've got much of a career to go back to. And I don't think I can face bumping into Alicia back at the station after all this. Once word gets round that I took two weeks off work only to fail to solve a homicide case I wasn't even assigned to, I'll be a laughing-stock.'

'You'll love it on Kembel,' said Glen. 'There's a gym. Neo-chromatic sauna. Fully heated swimming pool. The works.'

'I like swimming pools,' said the President, breaking off from his folk song and rejoining the conversation for a moment. 'As it happens, I ran for president on the platform of re-tiling the municipal swimming pool. If only I'd stuck to that. Me and my stupid dreams.' He started to cry quietly onto Misha's shoulder. 'You know, I really thought that one day we'd be able to turn the advertising hoarding on. That was what I *really* wanted. It would have been a powerful symbol of how the inhabitants of Gippsworld were finally worthy of targeted marketing strategies.'

Misha put down his milkshake mid-gulp. He turned to the President, and fixed him with a serious look. 'Our giant floating advertising hoarding. Does it work?'

The President shrugged.

'I guess. Never had cause to actually test it. I mean, one of the more poorly thought out aspects of the project was that the thing would cost a fortune to run, even for a few minutes. We can barely afford to pay the electricity bill as it is.'

'Listen, guys, don't go just yet,' Misha said, jumping up off the bar stool, his face suddenly animated. 'I think I've got a *plan*.'

Chapter Fourteen

The next morning the entire population of Gippsworld – along with Phoebe, Glen, and the Gollancz Senior Head of Marketing – huddled by the entrance to the mineshaft. They shivered in the perma-drizzle and tetchily complained to each other about what could be so important that they had to be out of bed at this time of day. Misha stood on an old packing crate, cleared his throat and waved.

'Hello,' he said. 'I'd like to thank you all for coming, even though I realise most of you are here because you didn't have anything else to do now that you're unemployed and destitute.'

Some of the Gippsworldians loudly wondered why the speeches directed at them always had to start on such a negative note.

'I know we normally have city meetings in the municipal centre,' Misha continued, 'but seeing as that's being repurposed as an abattoir by the new owners, this seemed the obvious place, given that it's our only real landmark. I'd especially like to thank the Head of Marketing from the Gollancz publishing group for taking time out of his busy schedule to be with us.'

The man in the white suit waved, yawned and looked at his watch.

'As you know, GABAN Corp have offered us the generous opportunity to all go back to our old jobs as pig farmers, though this would be as unpaid interns working on what is now their land. Of course, pig farming on Gippsworld has recently become a vital cog in their drugs production business, so this is, after a fashion, a rare chance to get a toehold in the competitive world of narcotics publishing. As I understand it they've even offered free surgery to fit us all with nutrient pipes, to negate the need for us to take a lunch break. Is that right?'

The Senior Head of Marketing nodded. Some of the more easily impressed Gippsworldians applauded.

'However, thrilled though we are with this offer, I am here today to make a counter offer. My proposal is this: that the publishers recognise that they took unfair advantage of our natural trusting natures and surprisingly low IQ scores, hand back the deeds to our pig farms and leave Gippsworld forever. In return we offer nothing but our gratitude and a solemn promise that no more will be said about the whole sorry business.'

The Senior Head of Marketing folded his arms and arched an eyebrow. 'Really?' he said, laughing. '*That*'s your counter offer?'

'It is, yes.'

'Well, I am afraid that on behalf of my company, I must regretfully decline.'

'I thought you would probably say that,' said Misha, with a sad nod. He turned to the President, who was sitting on a chair off to one side.

'Mister President, could you do the honours?'

The President got to his feet, saluted a bit pointlessly, did his noble middle-distance stare thing again, and then pressed the button on a small control pad.

The faint echoing crackle of a trillion circuits warming up for the very first time made everybody jump. There was a brief, distant hum. The crowd craned their heads towards the clouds. There was a pause, and then, high above them, up in the troposphere, the three-mile wide advertising hoarding blazed on, the countless hyper-LEDs that made up the screen all suddenly pulsing with their maximum wattage.

It was as if Gippsworld suddenly had a second, less embarrassed sun.

The Senior Head of Marketing stared up at it, puzzled. Every single Gippsworldian stared up at it as well. They gawped at the first bright sky they'd ever seen. Marvelling, they looked at each other happily, and then they quickly looked away again, because it turned out most Gippsworldians looked slightly better in the gloom. The light from the billboard fell with an ersatz heavenly glow on the mineshaft. It fell on the spaceport. It fell on the claggy fields of mud and on the municipal centre and on the closed-down artisanal bakery. For a minute, nothing much happened.

Then, like a dawn chorus comprised of gloopy 'pops', every single pig on Gippsworld exploded.

* * *

'Did you just wipe out an entire species?' said Glen, shielding his eyes against the glare and fishing about in his pocket for a pair of shades. 'Did you just commit mass pig genocide?'

Misha looked a bit guiltily at the ground. 'I guess I did, yes.'

Everybody went very quiet for a moment.

'Don't worry, I think genocide is okay, ethically speaking, so long as the creatures aren't very lovable,' said Phoebe reassuringly. 'I'm pretty sure I read that somewhere.'

'WHAT DID YOU DO?' screamed the Senior Head of Marketing, who had suddenly stopped seeming quite so urbane and had turned a shade of pink that didn't go with his phosphorescent cravat at all. 'WHAT THE HELL DID YOU DO?'

'He killed your pigs, bro,' said Glen.

'Do you have ANY idea what I've gone through?' the man raved, grabbing Misha by the collar and shaking him. 'Do you have any CLUE what it's been like, getting this *fucking* assignment?' He threw his hat on the ground and stamped on it in a fury. 'Two months I've been here. Two months! It should have been a three-day turn around. And we've been working on our campaign for SIX YEARS. The sponsorship deals ... the non-refundable media buy-ins ...'

He slumped onto a Gippsworld rock, held his face in his hands, and babbled softly to himself about his job issues.

'I'm sorry you've had a bit of a setback,' said Misha. 'But obviously there's nothing here for you now, so perhaps you'd best be off. I'm sure Vitali would be happy to drive you to the spaceport.'

The Senior Head of Marketing squinted at him. He breathed deeply, held his own wrist and counted out his pulse for a few seconds. Then he reached into his suit jacket and pulled out a dangerous-looking cylinder, evil black and yellow stripes running down its length. Most of the Gippsworldians, who had been enjoying the scene up to that point, chose this moment to remember some other work they had on, and slunk away in different directions. The publisher levelled the cylinder at the trio of Misha, Phoebe and Glen. They edged backwards, but found themselves right at the lip of the formerly-famous Gippsworld mineshaft.

'I've really had it with you *hicks*,' said the Senior Head of Marketing.

'Hey, is that a Mallowiser4000?' said Glen.

'It's a Face Repurposer.'

'Oh,' said Glen, disappointed. 'I was hoping you'd go with Mallowiser4000.'

'They were both good names,' said the Senior Head of Marketing. 'It was a toss-up.'

'Sure, no, don't worry, I understand. But listen, buddy,' said Glen, holding his hands up. 'I'm not really anything to do with this whole enterprise. I'm the innocent hired gun with no vested interest. So if it's all the same, I'll step out of the current imbroglio and let you guys work it out.'

Glen shuffled off to the side. 'Sorry,' he whispered to Phoebe. 'I just really like my face. I don't want it repurposed. Whereas your face, though kind of nice, could probably be rebuilt even better than before, if it came to it. It's a very illegible situation.'

'You are so fucking dumped,' said Phoebe.

'Don't be like that. Why are you being like that?'

'PROBABLY ON THE RAG,' said the hen.

'Oh, that's *it*.'

Phoebe, overcome with the unexpected calm born from having a really terrible day, suddenly dived sideways into the mud, and in one fluid movement scooped up the hen by its neck and flung it into the air. The hen squawked, alarmed. Then, with a quick internal adjustment to her cybernetic power output, Phoebe booted it right at the Senior Head of Marketing. Caught off guard, he clumsily set off the Face Repurposer at point blank range, and got a big cloud of feathers and beak bits in his face for his trouble. He gazed down at his ruined suit, and turned an even grimmer shade of purple than he had been before. Phoebe took advantage of his momentary lapse of concentration to leap back up and smack him round the head with her sonic truncheon. He crumpled to the ground in a heap.

'You're under arrest for threatening a police officer – and hen murder,' said Phoebe, clipping some handcuffs on him.

'Hen murder isn't a thing,' said the Senior Head of Marketing.

'I could make it a thing,' said the President, who had been watching from behind his chair. 'That's one of the perks of being president.'

The few Gippsworldians who hadn't already drifted off – not really sure what was going on, but sensing a happy ending – broke into a spontaneous round of applause.

Phoebe bowed, dusted herself down, turned to Misha and beamed.

'That was great!' said Misha. 'I really didn't like that hen.'

'You were great too!' said Phoebe. 'Earlier, I mean, the stuff with the advertising hoarding and the pigs.'

'Oh, well. Actually, on that note, there's something else.' Misha grinned sheepishly. He pointed up at the billboard. Then he gave a swift thumbs up to the President, who hit another button on his control panel. The blaze of light gradually dimmed, and formed itself into words. Kilometre-high letters started to spell out a sentence:

MISHA
BULGAKOV
LOVES
PHOEBE
CLAG

Phoebe, slack-jawed in disbelief, stared at it. A few members of the crowd made 'wooo' noises. Somewhere a strained plasma generator fizzed. Phoebe grimaced.

'Too much?' said Misha, suddenly anxious.

'A little bit,' said Phoebe, with an apologetic nod. 'It's … it's kind of over the top.'

'Yes, even I can see that just comes across as quite *creepy*,' said Glen, shaking his head.

Misha deflated. 'In his book, *Be My Hyperspace – Wooing Across The Spacelanes*, Cliff Ganymede says bold romantic gestures in public settings are one of the best ways of impressing a girl. Like a bee's waggle dance.'

'You should stop reading those books, Misha. They're not very good.'

There was a long, difficult pause.

'Well,' said the President. 'This is awkward.'

Phoebe and Misha did their best not to look at each other. They hovered by the edge of the mineshaft as the rain kept coming down in slabs. Somewhere deep inside Phoebe a neural link misfired. A tiny hydraulic motor whirred. Her cybernetic leg spasmed. And for the second time, though with the power now turned right up to its maximum, she kicked Misha hard in the shin.

He hopped backwards. He wobbled. Then – almost in slow motion, as it seemed to the onlookers, his mouth making a soundless, surprised 'O' – he lost his footing on the slippery Gippsworld mud. Phoebe gasped, frozen to the spot in horror. She watched Misha crash through the poor-quality safety barrier and tumble over the edge of the fifth-deepest mineshaft in the galaxy. He disappeared into the bowels of the planet, spinning helplessly towards his certain doom.

'Whoops,' said the Senior Head of Marketing.

'Oh dear,' said the President.

'You should probably think about getting that fixed,' said Glen.

Chapter Fifteen

'Listen, lover,' said the Thargoid Queen, propping herself up on a pillow and exhaling a languorous, noxious gas cloud through one of her mucus vents. 'It's a crying shame things didn't work out with you and the police lady, but at least we found each other.'

She extended her glistening proboscis and ruffled Misha's hair. Misha winced. He couldn't really remember how they'd started dating. 'It's odd,' he hissed out of the side of his mouth, leaning over towards the President, who for some reason was in bed with them. 'As a type, I don't usually go for clacking mandibles and chitinous exoskeletons and deathly, inhuman compound eyes.'

'But you really *get* each other. Isn't that the important thing?' said the President. 'You like all the same films. You've got the same taste in soft furnishings. Besides which, she's smart! And *royalty*.'

'I guess,' whispered Misha. 'I'm just not sure I'm into her in *that* way. Does that sound shallow?'

'After we copulate, I will devour your head,' said the Thargoid Queen, giving him a saucy unblinking stare, 'as is the tradition amongst my race.'

Misha sighed. 'Can't mess with tradition, I suppose.'

* * *

He opened his eyes, and found that he was still in bed, but the Thargoid Queen seemed to have morphed into a bunch of tubes and a drip and an uncomfortable catheter. He could smell antiseptic and chip fat.

'Where am I?' he said, his voice coming out like a croak.

'Hey! You're awake!' Phoebe exclaimed, tearing her gaze away from something on the holographic display above her. She was sitting in a chair next to his bed, magazines and empty noodle pots piled up in her lap. 'How are you feeling? Don't try to move too much – you shattered quite a lot of bones. You're in the *Jim Bergerac* hospital pod. It's next to the Omar Sharif Jazz Lounge, which is why it smells of chip fat. Your health insurance is pretty lousy, I'm afraid.'

'What happened?' said Misha. He rubbed his eyes, trying to shake off a fog of painkillers. 'That mineshaft is two miles deep. There's no way I could have survived the fall.'

'You caught a break!' Phoebe grinned at him. 'You were saved by an entire population's complete lack of artistic talent.'

'I don't think I understand that statement,' said Misha.

'Remember how I told you I kept on finding ships that were *supposed* to be transporting Gippsworld artworks but which didn't have anything in their holds? Well, now I know why. The marketing guy pretty much spilled the beans on the whole deal. Not the first time they've tried to pull this scam, you see.' She leant over and fed him a grape. 'Basically, the publisher's plan was pretty simple: they turn up, start an economic bubble – tulips, hats, art, whatever – and use that to get the locals to sell them whatever the *really* valuable resource is for chump change. Usually it's a breeze, by all accounts. They plant a few articles in trend-setting publications, get a couple of movers and shakers to endorse the "product", and the fad hungry populace of the galaxy do the rest. Except, this time, it didn't work.'

'What do you mean "it didn't work"? People went mad for Gippsworld art.'

'No. You see, it turns out the Gippsworldians were all so *preternaturally untalented* that even the art world – the art world, for crying out loud! – even they couldn't be persuaded to collect the stuff. So our poor marketing guy, sweating it by this point, had to bribe all these traders to ship the stuff out. Lucky for him Gippsworld was daft enough to pay for it themselves, via this ridiculous Outsider Art Fund. But anyhow, all these traders were being bribed to export it, but they knew that they didn't have anywhere to export it *to*. So, to save a bit of time and fuel, they all just started dumping it down the mineshaft when nobody was looking. Tons of the stuff! So much, they clogged up the hole. And as a result, instead of falling two miles to your certain doom, you fell about a hundred feet onto a cushion of mud sculptures. Apparently you landed directly on top of *Prometheus, Reclining, Contemplates The Howling Void*, and one of its knobbly bits got embedded in your spleen. The bonus of all this is that I got to solve my Case of the Missing Cargo. Which is going to get written up in the departmental newsletter as Investigation of the Month! That's kind of a big deal, and has put Alicia's nose properly out of joint.'

'What about the Ganymede case?' said Misha, struggling to sit up.

Phoebe shrugged. 'Still down as a suicide, officially. But the marketing guy is serving ten years, after the Gippsworld President retroactively made hen murder a Class One Offence. And look, you're famous.' She passed him a magazine.

'AREA MAN DESTROYS ENTIRE SPECIES' read the headline, '"KNUCKLE DOWN" DRUG MARKETING CAMPAIGN CANCELLED AT ENORMOUS EXPENSE, GABAN CONGLOMERATE SHARE PRICE TUMBLES.'

'I still feel bad about the pigs,' said Misha, looking at the magazine sadly. 'I mean, what's Gippsworld going to do now? Without pigs there's just the methane. And that's, you know, *methane*. Nobody is really crying out for it.'

'Come on, Misha, you stopped half the galaxy topping themselves! Give yourself some credit. And besides – tourism is through the roof,' she wiped a hand across the magazine and the headline changed to 'GIPPSWORLD GENOCIDE A-GO-GO' above a picture of the smiling President cutting a ribbon. 'It turns out people really DO like to visit places where famous atrocities have happened. You can buy "Butcher of Gippsworld" tea towels now with a photograph of you on them.'

'Oh, well. That's nice, I suppose.'

'And that's not all: one of the news crews covering the pig genocide noticed that the stain in my shirt looked a lot like Vladimir Putin's face. It's being hailed as some sort of miracle.'

'You mean like a Virgin-Mary-appearing-on-a-Taco sort of deal?'

'Exactly! I donated it to the newly created Gippsworld Miracle Stain museum, and now there are queues round the block to see it. It's a double whammy.'

'How's, um, Glen doing?'

Phoebe wrinkled her nose, and went back to concentrating on some strange flickering shapes on the holographic display. 'He's given up pirating for the moment, and his restaurant idea, and has turned his hand to recording an album of acoustic songs about how much he misses his dead hen. Marty Zeevon is going to represent him. Says it's going to be big, but I'm not so sure.'

Misha shifted around uncomfortably. He bit his lip. 'Did you change your mind about … you know, *us*?'

'Not really,' said Phoebe, giving him a sisterly pat on the head. 'It's still hard to see you as a viable sexual partner after your appallingly misjudged billboard stunt.'

'Fair enough,' said Misha, with a resigned nod.

'But oh, yeah – I almost forgot, I've got something for you,' Phoebe reached down under the little table by the side of his bed, and pulled out the Lenslok box. 'The guys up in IT support managed to crack it. Turns out Lenslok technology is, rather than being impregnable, actually *rubbish*. Who knew!'

'So what's in it?'

'Open it.'

With a little difficulty Misha reached across, and took the box from her. He clicked open the catch and pushed back the lid.

'Oh,' he said, peering inside.

He pulled out a heavy beige rectangle, about the size of a large food printer. It had an incomprehensible-looking keyboard. A hieroglyph of a bird in one corner was the only bit of decoration. It made his hand tingle, because the entire thing was encased in a preservation field, like those he'd felt around old comics in museums.

'Congratulations,' said Phoebe. 'You are now guilty of antiquity smuggling. There's usually a ten credit fine, but I think I can let you off with a warning for a first time offence.'

'What is it? Some sort of loom? It looks ancient.'

'Almost. It's a primitive computer. About a thousand years old.'

'Wow. Is it valuable?'

'No, not particularly. Probably the only reason it was being smuggled by your mysterious platinum blonde is it fell foul of Placet-B's nostalgia law.'

160

'Well,' said Misha, putting the box down again. 'That's disappointing.'

'Yes, but them's the breaks – oh god*damn*.' Phoebe suddenly punched the arm of her chair and glowered at the hologram.

Misha looked up at it. A few lo-fi, sketchy polygons were bobbing about. 'What are you *doing*?'

'Sorry. It's some dumb old game, or flight simulator software or something, I started playing it whilst I was waiting for you to come round. Guess they used it for training the early cosmonauts. I found it in an online archive when I was doing a background search to work out exactly what that thing was,' Phoebe jabbed her thumb at the blocky antique computer. 'It's really crazy. Everything's just … *flat*. I can't get the hang of it. You have a go.'

She handed him her control pad.

'You know,' said Misha, clicking a few buttons randomly, 'a near death experience like falling into a mineshaft makes you have something of an epiphany.'

'How so?'

'You suddenly look at life in a whole new way. The sheer wonder of it all.'

'Oh god. You're sounding like Glen.'

'No. I mean it. It's like I've been given a second chance. Seriously, Phoebe, from this point on I'm going to really make a go of things.'

'Okay,' said Phoebe, frowning. 'But, doesn't that sort of fly in the face of everything we discovered about the cold brutality of the universe? The sheer unremitting unfairness of the system? The pointlessness of trying?'

Misha pulled a face. 'How do we really *know* there wasn't some sort of chemical side effect to Knuckle Down? We don't! Besides which, even it was true that things didn't work out for *those* people, I don't think it's necessarily true for *me*. I just haven't ever given my full potential a chance.'

'That editor would probably tell you it's that kind of deluded thinking which is the whole problem in the first place.'

Misha cursed as something went wrong on the screen above him.

'I'm a changed man. It's a brand new Misha. And not because of some stupid pill.'

'So. What's the first step towards the new you?'

'For a start, I'm going to write that novel. This past week has given me a lot of material. And I'm going to do it right now. Not tomorrow, not in a little while. Right this instant. No more messing about. No more procrastinating.'

Phoebe frowned as the two dimensional image above Misha's head flashed.

'I think you've got to try to line up the hole in the polygon with the cross hairs.'

'Yes, thanks, I've worked that out.'

They sat there in silence for a while. Phoebe yawned.

'Can I have another go? It's quite boring just watching.'

'Sure,' said Misha, starting the game up again. 'Just give me another ten minutes.'